HUNTER'S MOON

Also by David Devereux from Gollancz:

Eagle Rising

HUNTER'S MOON

David Devereux

This edition published in Great Britain in 2017
by Gollancz.

First published in Great Britain in 2009
by Gollancz
an imprint of the Orion Publishing Group Ltd
Carmelite House, 50 Victoria Embankment
London EC4Y 0DZ

An Hachette UK Company

1 3 5 7 9 10 8 6 4 2

A CIP catalogue record for this book
is available from the British Library.

ISBN 978 1 473 22186 4

Typeset by Input Data Services Ltd, Somerset

Printed by CPI Group (UK) Ltd, Croydon, CR0 4YY

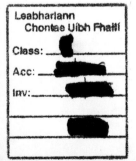

MIX
Paper from
responsible sources
FSC® C104740
www.fsc.org

www.orionbooks.co.uk
www.gollancz.co.uk

A Note From the Author

I've done my best to keep things as realistic as possible on the material level, and gratefully acknowledge the help I've had with that from a number of people who would prefer to remain nameless. There is, however, one point that I'd like to make perfectly clear:

ALL THE MAGIC IN THIS BOOK IS FAKE.
I MADE IT UP.

The basic principles are sound, but since I don't want anyone out there trying to do the things that Jack does, I assembled his methods from a wide variety of incompatible systems; so while it *looks* like the real thing, it's the magical equivalent of a chocolate fireguard. Don't try this at home, kids. Don't try any of the bits that include brainwashing, torture or violence either. Please, play nice. As for the sex, just remember the three magic words: safe, Sane and Consensual.

There are a number of people that I *can* name who I should also like to thank:

Steve Jackson, for talking me into writing another book.

Simon Spanton, my editor, for taking a chance on the scary-looking bald guy with strange ideas.

Robert Caskie, my agent, for helping to keep my head

attached and continuing to stick with me during my adventures in print.

Liz Taylor, my Glamorous Assistant, for services above, beyond and bizarre.

Cat Vincent, for the Broom Cupboard.

Roger Burton West, for giving this tale a title, reminding me of my anatomy and picking nits in general. Also the legendary Chris Bell for refreshing my memory on several parts of the English language that had slipped out of my head since school, and Jolane Abrams for general reading services.

Finally, two young ladies of my acquaintance, to whom I shall refer as 'A' and 'E', for being kind enough to act as technical consultants in some of the more delicate moments of the story.

This book is dedicated to everyone who thought I could do it.

Kind regards,
David Devereux
London, 6 September 2006.

Introit
The New Forest

Another night in the sticks. The woods are, as the poet said, dark and deep. And wet – pissing it down, in fact. About fifteen feet or so away, I can see a couple of guys chatting under a tree: sentries taking shelter and wagging their chins as they have since time immemorial. They shouldn't be, of course. They should be walking the perimeter and keeping an eye out for trouble. Not that I'm complaining; it's a combination of the weather and their complete lack of attention that's allowed me to get this close to them in the first place. Moving slowly nearer, roughly ten feet out now, close enough to hear them discussing a mate's wife. Seems one of these naughty boys has been entertaining her in a way her husband wouldn't necessarily like. Bad puppy, no biscuit. Frankly, I couldn't give a damn. I've already got them marked down as bad people, and shagging somebody else's wife is the least of the reasons I can think of. Six feet away now. I can see the whites of their eyes, smell the dodgy whiff coming off their kit and am now learning far too much about how a rather dignified suburban housewife likes to be tied up and violated with kitchen tools that she then uses to cook hubby's dinner. I'm about ready to stand up and give them a bollocking for not doing their jobs properly, but it's a yin/yang thing: get some good, get some bad, and the game balances out in the end. Time to hurry up and wait. Trouble is I'm more in the 'hurry up' camp than the 'wait'.

A few more minutes of details I really don't want to hear, and they eventually remember where they left their respective clues. Shagger wanders off and starts taking a turn around the area – obviously not expecting trouble, equally obvious he'd prefer not to meet any. As his mate watches him walk out of sight, I'm slowly rising from the bushes with a knife in my hand. Easy as pie and over before he even knows I'm there. A little loose brush to keep him out of sight for a while, then back into hiding. Shagger reappears after five minutes; he obviously hasn't bothered with much in the way of paying attention to his environment and while I'm grateful to him, in some part of the back of my head I'm seriously hacked off at the bloody awful job of sentrying he's done. To cap his sins, he assumes his mate's gone for a pee in the bushes and whispers an off-colour joke into the shrubbery next to me. He goes on to assume that the rustling coming out of that shrubbery is his mate, and does nothing to make his weapon ready in case it isn't. He's still reaching for it as he hits the deck, and I start camouflaging his mortal remains.

No point scavenging from the dead here – I've got what I need for the moment and wouldn't trust their kit anyway. Judging from what I've already seen of them I wouldn't expect their maintenance schedule to be any better than their performance as sentries. Move on, deal with the next thing, get through the gig and then we can head home for tea and medals.

Moving quietly through undergrowth is a skill, and a state of mind. The world is your friend: the trees, the bracken, the birds – everything is your best friend and wishes you well in your progress. Feet carefully placed with each step, a certain combination of confidence and timidity that can't be adequately described. It's one of those things that you either can do, or you can't. I learned it from a miserable old git called Sergeant Walters during my infiltration training in Wales. I've heard that Wales is a lovely place, picturesque and blessed with a fine climate. In my experience it's a Hell where the weather's permanently cold, raining or both – except when it snows. Then it gets *bloody* cold. But it's a good place to learn infantry skills, especially when you've got someone like Wally to teach you.

But this is not a time for reminiscing, there's a job on.

The objective's in sight now, a cave-opening with one guard outside it. A quick look from another angle lets me know that nobody can see him from inside, so he's fair game as far as I'm concerned. Close in to the edge of the tree line – about ten feet. Inside knife range, so pause, pick the moment and throw.

Taking someone with a knife isn't like the movies. They don't wave their arms, or scream, or any of that pantomime nonsense. You get a sort of huffing sound as the impact empties the air out of their lungs, then a gentle gurgling noise as blood moves in to replace it. The facial expression is best described as a cross between surprise and confusion – both of which strike me as perfectly understandable under the circumstances.

Slipping across to the mouth of the cave, I retrieve my knife and conceal another metaphorical notch on the hilt.

The cave's warm, and I can hear activity inside. Not that I'm surprised. It's been an easy run so far and I know that isn't going to last for ever. Shedding my ghillie suit (an hour's painstaking work with a net and some local foliage), I move inside ninja style, using my now matt-black gear to slide between shadows. I blink a few times to help my eyes adjust to the new light level, one eye at a time so I don't lose sight of the world around me.

In front of me is an obvious supply area. There are boxes of kit stacked against one wall and a passageway leading into the hill. From further in I can hear voices – sounds as if the show's started in there, so I'd better stop farting about and get on with what I'm here to do: unpacking the charges, setting them up around the mouth of the cave, the area I'm in and the passageway. Ten small but potent packets of C-4 plastic explosive with a radio detonator, set to fire in sequence. It takes longer than I'd like but there's no way around that. Stop, look, think, place, check. No short cuts: hurrying can get you killed. Now the whole front of this cave is set to collapse well enough to ensure that anyone trapped inside will die of old age before they manage to dig their way out, which is just the way I want it.

Onward, ever onward . . .

Moving a little faster now, letting the increased noise cover the soft sound of my footsteps. Knife in my right hand, ready for when it's needed. Keeping my breathing under control, slow and steady despite the adrenaline rushing through my system like an express train. I can feel the pistol under my left arm, lengthened beyond what I consider reasonable by the silencer. I don't like guns, they're loud and messy. Can't avoid them, though. Sometimes you don't get a choice.

Another guard, this one with his back to me. Swift and silent. Conceal the body.

Time for some maths. Four men down so far. I already know to expect seventeen in the main chamber. At least two more, then – this kind of outfit seems to like prime numbers and the next one's twenty-three. After that it's twenty-nine – so I'm hoping for the former. Nobody's going home tonight except me, and six extra kills would just be annoying.

At the same time I'm trying to figure out just how big these caves are. I know where the main chamber is and how to get there, but intel didn't bring back much else and I've not really had a chance to recce the place at all. As a result there are more question marks on this job than I would be inclined to approve of. But they're paying me money and if I spend any more time sitting here with my thumb up my arse I'll soon be worrying about something else entirely.

Judging from what I can hear I'm going to need to get a move on. Things in the main chamber are starting to get a little louder, and it won't be long before anything I do is going to be academic. If those silly sods outside had been doing their jobs properly and not left me sitting around, it would have been easier to take them and get in here on schedule. But then if I could tell the opposition what to do, I'd be sat at home with a mug of cocoa, rather than prowling around out here, cold, wet and four bodies into what the tabloids would undoubtedly call a 'blood-crazed killing spree' or something equally silly.

This area's larger, better equipped. Street clothes on hangers, spare weapons, field kit: all the comforts a cell like this could hope for, along with the entrance to the main chamber. Trouble is, it's unguarded. Not good. That puts an extra punter on my 'unpleasant surprises' list . . .

. . . And here he is. Obviously been to the loo, judging by the way he's still doing up his flies and has his weapon slung. Hooray for small mercies. A flat punch to the throat, crushing the trachea; a nice little move that suffocates him while rendering him unable to scream. Point of knife under the jaw and thrust slightly upwards, through to sever the spinal cord at the back. Messy, but effective.

Which is of course the point were it all goes to shitrags. No chance to hide this one before his mate walks in – and we've finally found our first grown-up. Switched on, tooled up and very unhappy to see me. Moving fast, I step into close range, knock his rifle aside as he's bringing it up and throw my left fist at his throat. He blocks. Reset my attack into an elbow at his ear. He moves his head and takes it on the skull – painful but not incapacitating. Following in with the knife in my right hand – a nice slice on the neck, but nowhere important. He plants the butt of his rifle in my guts, which would have hurt a lot more without the body armour. Twitching to the side, kicking his knee, hearing a loud crack as the joint snaps in a direction it wasn't designed to bend and he goes down. A knee on his chest, followed by his own glove in his mouth. I need this one alive. In fact, judging by what I can hear in the next room, this poor bastard is my only chance of completing the job and getting my sweet self safely home.

Looking him in the eye: 'Anyone else out here?' He

shakes his head: *No.* I breathe a sigh of relief. The last thing I need at this point is half a dozen other bastards wandering around ready to interrupt me. This is the complicated bit, and a distraction would be worse now than when I was setting the charges.

Out with the plastic handcuffs; secure his wrists and ankles. Onto his side, out with the knife. A single cut from groin to neck, opening his outfit like a zip. Now he's wondering what's going on, and then the light dawns in his eyes and he starts struggling.

Next door, things have reached a climax. Now chummy here really is my only chance. Check his pulse, find it a little unsteady but strong; he's got a good heart, as they say.

Looking down at him: 'Sorry, mate. Wrong place, wrong time. Serves you right for playing with the bad boys.'

Out with the book, find the right page – carefully marked in case I ended up here. Start reading. Forcing out my clunky Latin as I bring the knife into position . . .

They say the way to a man's heart is through his stomach, and they're almost right. Personally I prefer to go in just above the stomach, specifically just under the ribcage. Upward angle to cut through the diaphragm, being careful not to go too deep and nick the pericardial sac, and then across in one good, firm cut to get it done as quickly as you can. It's not exactly a surprise to see my new friend go into shock at this point. I certainly would in his position.

In with the hand, up inside the chest cavity. Fingers sliding between lung and pericardium. Finding the aortic arch – the top of the heart. Taking as firm a grip as I can, since you only get one chance at this – trying to concentrate as I keep spooling off the Latin. Feeling his heart fluttering against the palm of my right hand. Reaching the correct point, give it one swift pull and then I'm standing with an old book in one hand and a heart running through its last couple of beats in the other.

Time for the icky bit.

Finishing the incantation, lifting the heart, biting into it as it beats its last.

Next door, Hell breaks loose. Literally. The demon that's just arrived in there suddenly realises that he's free to do whatever he wants, and decides to make full use of the happy surprise. Oddly enough, this seems to involve expressing his quite considerable displeasure at being summoned from wherever he was by what he considers to be the evolutionary equivalent of a not particularly bright amoeba. There are sounds of chewing among the screams.

Now all I have to do is send him home. Swallowing, throwing the heart aside and wiping my hand on my trousers, I pull the holy water out of my pocket and dump it over my head with a quick prayer. Insta-Baptism, my mate Dead Geoff calls it. It's as good a name as any. Another incantation from the book as I reach into my webbing and pull out the silver knife, blessed by a cooperative bishop of our acquaintance.

A quick peek into the cave shows me the back of the thing they've summoned. At least I think it's the back – it doesn't seem to have a face and looks as if it's, um, *consuming* someone on the other side of the room. Throw the knife as I say the prayer and thank every god I can think of when it hits. I don't get to see what happens next as I'm already running like Jesse Owens for the way out, but the sound . . .

Imagine a thousand fingernails scraping down a thousand blackboards. Now get your favourite DJ (I personally dig Mr C) to mix that onto a thousand choirboys being buggered with soldering irons. It's worse, way worse: and louder than a jet engine. But I don't care, because I'm still running. In fact, I'm still running when I get outside, trigger the explosives and bring that hill down on the whole stinking mess as the thing gets sent back to wherever it came from.

I really fucking hate full moons.

Chapter One

My name is unimportant, but you can call me Jack. I'm a musician by choice, a magician by profession and a bastard by disposition.

I'd been doing the magic thing for about five years when they found me. They said I had a talent, that I was smart enough and fit enough and enough of a shit that I could serve my country in a way most people never even get to hear about. And I *did* want to serve my country, *didn't I*?

I didn't really want to contemplate what might happen if I said no.

So I caved in and went to a big old pile in the country where I learned a lot more about magic, and guns, and all sorts of other ways to ruin a bloke's day. They made me fitter and sent me off to play with the Army – generally turned me into Mr Bastard with a wand and no trouble using it or any other method to get my way.

Then they put me to work. I've been doing this for a while now, and the job isn't exactly something I'd recommend. But the hours are all right, the pay's fantastic and you get to be awfully friendly with as many impressionable young witches as you can handle, so I suppose it could be worse.

I'd had a call from the Boss summoning me to the office

for a briefing. We don't go in much, for obvious reasons, but the department has offices all over the place for things like this, mostly disguised as storerooms. Well, do you honestly *know* what's behind that door down the corridor marked 'Supplies'? Didn't think so. I wouldn't recommend looking, though. Just in case. There's only one way to reliably stop people from talking, and we don't like being talked about. Do the maths, and keep your nose out. That way you'll avoid having someone like me demonstrating the ways we have of ruining *your* day.

Today's office was another janitorial supply facility near the top of Regent Street in an anonymous building where you don't need ID to get in or an escort when you do. We love places like this. I headed past the lift and up the stairs to the third floor (an old habit), along the corridor and up to the unmarked door. One key fits all the locks we use, and as I let myself in the Boss was waiting.

I haven't got a clue what my boss is called. We were introduced with the phrase 'Welcome to my department' and no one's ever seen fit to tell me since. Suits me; I suppose it's a security thing. You can't reveal what you don't know. It's not as if you'd notice him on the train or anything; he's one of those grey little men you see everywhere. Five feet ten, thinning hair, bland face, glasses, doesn't wear the old school tie, but inside there is the most heartless shit I've ever seen. He could give Himmler a run for his money, that one. Looks a bit like Himmler, too, now I come to think about it. Obviously a career desk jockey, since his dislike for field staff is palpable; I can only imagine that putting up with us seemed like a good career move or something.

The desk was the same as every other desk in every other office, empty apart from a green-shaded lamp, two telephones – one black, one white – and the envelope containing the case file. The Boss was sitting behind the desk looking at me as if I'd kept him waiting for an hour. A quick check of the clock on the wall told me I was on time.

'Morning, sir.' The reaction I got was hardly worth the effort. Staring at me as if I was something nasty on a microscope slide, he pointed at a chair in front of the desk. He sat behind it, of course, and there was an empty chair to my side. He opened the envelope, removed a red folder and laid it open on the desk.

Red folders mean trouble. I don't like red folders. That last little trip to the New Forest had come in a red folder.

'The Enlightened Sisterhood. Heard of it?' No pleasantries, straight to business.

'Yes, sir, it's your standard Goddess-worshipping, man-hating, we-know-everything-because-we're-women type outfit. Fairly standard, as I recall; about as much use as any other dumb supremacist outfit.'

'Maybe not. Word is they're planning something. I don't know what, but I want to. Once I know what's going on, you'll get further orders. It's possible they may need to be closed down.'

'You mean you want me to walk in there and slaughter them all.' The Boss was a master of euphemism. The idea of me arranging blackmail appeared to unsettle him, let alone telling me to slot somebody. He could order it; he just didn't like to say it so bluntly. He seemed to be under the impression that I just made problems go away because he didn't like them. A terror behind a desk, I'd give him five seconds tops in the real world. I enjoy yanking his chain at moments like this – reminding him of exactly what he's asking for. The black look I got for my trouble was worth it.

'That remains to be seen. Background.' He almost threw the folder at me.

'One problem. I don't think I'll be able to ... penetrate the Sisterhood. If you see my point. I don't think my charm's going to do it for them.'

'No. You'll be back-up for the infiltrator. Liaise, share data, watch her back. The usual thing.'

'You want me to what? Do I look like a babysitter? Why me?'

'Frankly, because you won't have a problem with killing two dozen women when I tell you to. Too many people in this Service have scruples about that sort of thing. I may not like you; in fact, you may well be the most unpleasant man I've ever met. But you have your uses and this is one of them. So be a good boy and do as you're bloody well told. Understand?' A vein in his temple fluttered slightly. He didn't like explaining himself to the help – we were beneath him, and he liked to make sure we knew it. To be honest, I couldn't care less.

I shrugged. 'Yes, sir.'

'Right. For now the job is to find out what the hell's going on – action to be decided after we have all the facts. You're going in now so you'll have a cover if and when you're needed, and so there's a chance you might get a look at them before anything happens. Just establish the cover and keep your nose clean. Clear?'

'Crystal.'

There wasn't really anything else to say, so I pulled the safe house address out of the file, pocketed it, then closed the file and stuck it back on the desk.

'Good hunting,' said the Boss. It was traditional, rather than a genuine good wish. I got the hell out of there as fast as was decent and headed home to pack, pausing only to admire the well-toned backside of a cycle courier with more metal in her face than there is in my webbing as she bounced up the steps into the building as I left. I couldn't resist a smile, and she couldn't resist a sneer. I suppose I wasn't her type.

The next part was standard: back to my place in Archway and sort my kit out. There's stuff you want, stuff you don't and stuff that will be provided. Clothes, for example: the cover we'd be living might not match my tendency to wear jeans, Cat boots and leather jackets, so the office would have sorted out something more appropriate. But I'd still want my kit – knives, wand, a couple of ritual bits and pieces and my pistol. As an afterthought, I burned my electronic copies of the *Corpus Hermeticum* and the collected works of Crowley onto a DVD for reading on my laptop. There'd be plenty of sitting around on this gig, and I'd probably need a laugh. With my bag packed, I set the alarms and headed for the safe house where I'd meet the other agent and plan the job.

The Tube was busy, as usual; the Northern Line awful, as ever. If nothing else, it would be good to get out of London for a bit.

Safe house of the day turned out to be in Chelsea – a very nice two-bedroom place with a decent-sized living room. I worked out which room was mine and started unpacking, laying my kit out piece by piece on the bed-spread, checking each as I laid it out. I'd checked it as I packed, but you check and check again because that way you know it's going to work when you need it. Then I stripped my pistol down and cleaned it thoroughly. I had nothing else to do.

By the time evening had rolled round, all my kit was back in place and sparkling clean. I could have taken the lot on parade and had any sergeant major in the world buying me a beer for my trouble. Boredom was starting to cut in, though, so I started some t'ai chi and was halfway through my third round when the other half of the team arrived.

She was cute, in a boyish kind of way. Small, slim, mid-twenties at a guess. Cropped dark hair in a pixie cut. Looked a bit like Audrey Hepburn, in fact. The tight jeans showed her off nicely below the waist, but I couldn't form much of an opinion on the rest since there was a puffer jacket in the way. She dropped her bag on the floor and held her hand out.

'Pleased to meet you. I'm—'

'No names. Stick to cover. Safer for both of us.'

'Oh.'

'So I'm Bill Freeman, and you're Annie ...'

'Hargreaves. You're a bit paranoid, aren't you?'

'Yes.' I did my usual running paranoia check – yep, I could still breathe. 'I'm a firm believer in need-to-know. You don't need to know my real name, and if you did, it would only be a liability. Besides, if we only have one name apiece, there's no chance of a slip-up.' Not only that,

I thought, we don't get to be friends. The last thing I need is emotion getting in the way when I have to choose between you and the objective.

As we talked, she took the jacket off and draped it over the sofa. The top half went very well with what had already been examined. Putting all the facts together, I came to the inevitable conclusion: I would. Or at least I would if she wasn't company property.

While she moved into her room, I put the kettle on. While I may be fond of coffee, I live on tea. NATO standard – white, two sugars. The fridge had the usual collection of ready meals waiting for our attention. We were going to be here for a couple of days, and wouldn't want to leave until we were ready to go to work. I shouted to see if she was hungry and got an affirmative, so I stuck the top of the meat pile in the oven with the top of the prepared veg pile. Instant mash would bulk it out. Half an hour at gas mark 7, which seems to cook every ready meal in the world – especially the ones that say twenty minutes. Then I wandered back in with two mugs of tea to discover the Boss's assistant sitting on the sofa with a briefcase on his lap, having let himself in.

This was Piers. He was, to use a technical term, a prick. Snotty, superior and obviously thought that his father should have found him a job with MI5 or something equally glamorous – not dealing with the great deniable unwashed like us. Gentlemen might have staffed the department during the war, having it toe-to-toe with the Thule Gesellschaft, but the rarefied atmosphere of clubs and wood-panelled restaurants was a thing of the past. Like every other branch of the secret world, we were down and dirty. Piers quite obviously hated that. Personally I think working in the Broom Cupboard (our own name for the Service among field officers – it seemed apt) embarrassed him. It was *too* secret. Being stuck with a clearance most people don't even hear about means talking shop isn't an option, and it must have just killed him to see his fellow Oxbridge types able to hint at things to each other, make cosy little deals and generally enjoy belonging to the club. Odds were that if any of those privileged idiots found out what Piers did at the office, I'd be sent round to stop them from telling anyone else. It happened with MPs occasionally, which had the potential to be entertaining. Well, it's not often you can set one of them up as some kind of fetishist who chokes on the cucumber they're fellating, now, is it?

Enjoying the memory, then putting Piers in the rubber minidress instead, I smiled. He thought I was being friendly, the idiot.

'I've got your briefing files here, plus some of your equipment. Put a requisition in for the rest as you work out what you'll want.' He made it sound as if I was an idiot for not knowing what I'd want for a job I didn't have all the facts on yet. I resisted the urge to slap him. Fortunately he wasn't one for small talk, and he was as keen to be gone as I was to get rid of him. By the time Annie had sorted herself out he'd left and there was food of some description sitting on the table with our respective copies of the file next to it. We ate in silence, reading as we chewed.

The Enlightened Sisterhood had been formed in the sixties, it appeared, by a group of feminists who were sick of the patriarchal set-ups of the more established orders. They wanted to make the world safer, and help stop male aggression, and all the usual cobblers. In short it was yet another bunch of man-hating lesbians who thought having a dick made you Satan incarnate. They'd joined in all the usual things over the years – ineffectual protests at Greenham Common, marches for this and that, lots of sitting around in circles singing 'We Shall Overcome' and such. There was evidence of them helping a couple of American kids skip the Vietnam draft, but they'd been reasonably quiet apart from that.

Things changed in the early eighties. Sadie Hamilton, now the leader, joined up and immediately started politicising things seriously. She'd become a member of the Communist Party at university and was obviously the kind of red who wanted to kick Thatcher and everything she stood for to pieces. Republican, obviously. MI5 had started a file on her at the age of eighteen, and a synopsis was attached with a note saying we could have a copy of the whole thing if we wanted. I made a note to get it ASAP – the more data we had, the better. She'd gone on from there to take charge of the Sisterhood in 1990, and was flagged as one of the possible causes of Thatcher's sudden breakdown during the leadership election. They'd tried pulling the usual anti-government magic, of course – they all do – but the guys from the defence section had knocked those spells out of the air before they had a chance to do much more than sound pretty. What had brought them to our attention seriously was the time they'd tried pulling Boudicca back from the dead. Not cool. The counter-attack we slapped on that left one of them gibbering in the foetal position and another thinking she was Dido, Queen of Carthage. She might have been at some point for all I know, but not while she was supposed to be a housewife called Janet with two kids and no husband. It didn't stop them, of course. They were either too stupid or too fanatical to take the hint, and they'd come close to being marked for closing down permanently. Maybe we should have – it would have saved us some time.

They'd had a crack at bringing about Armageddon at the millennium, but there were so many idiots trying that trick that all they had managed to do was get in each other's way like a bunch of Keystone Cops. It was hilarious at the time – you couldn't move for dickheads in robes waving every kind of thing imaginable and chanting in badly accented Latin, Ancient Egyptian or pseudo-Atlantean. The entire crop of field officers, normally responsible for stopping that kind of nonsense, took the night off and got thoroughly plastered in a stately home out in the sticks.

Since then they'd gone a bit quiet. They were recruiting, but apparently not doing much. That could be thought of as them behaving, but it just didn't fit the pattern. With this kind of mob, quiet means trouble. Quiet means they're planning something.

Looking up from the file, I could see that Annie was almost as well; I headed off to grab another load of tea before we got to her part of the briefing.

'I've been inside for eighteen months now,' she said when I got back. 'There are about twenty-five of us in the group for rituals, meetings and stuff. We're just doing the usual – nature, seasons, women's things – nothing that would surprise you. Within that, there's an inner circle of nine who seem to be the hardcore. They only open up a slot when someone leaves, so that needs to be arranged. They definitely have a fondness for girls who like girls, if you know what I mean, and I've been letting some anarchist philosophy slip as I've been working my way in. Looking at the rest, I don't think I'd have much competition moving up at the moment.'

'Fine.' I laid out a selection of photographs: the current membership of the Sisterhood. 'Any preferences?' Annie pointed at a mean-faced woman in her thirties. Karen Thomas, a teacher – probably the most hated one in her school by the look of her.

'She'll do. We don't get on, so it won't do me any harm to have her out of the way for a bit.' Annie obviously didn't realise what she'd just done, but I decided not to enlighten her.

'Right. I'll take care of that, then.'

We spent the rest of the night going over the files again, with Annie adding her notes and observations about the people involved. We sorted how my cover would fit with hers, along with all the various contingency plans for things that could go wrong. She was under the impression that I was supposed to bring her back no matter what, and again I wasn't going to upset her with the ruder facts of life. If she thought I was coming for her she'd hold out longer, give me more time to work. No, I thought, I wasn't going to tell her about the sealed orders in my folder that marked her as expendable.

Chapter Two

Annie headed off early the next morning. She couldn't afford to be away for too long in case questions were asked. The shopping bags and receipts were reasonable efforts to cover her absence, provided by some nameless functionary of a sufficiently similar size and appearance. This suited me down to the ground, since I still had to arrange kit and sort out my end of the op. She'd probably be all right, I thought, but she was definitely a little more naive than the sort of people I'm used to working with. You'd have thought a year and a half undercover would have knocked some of that out of her, but according to the file this was her first job for us and she'd not had much contact – just what was necessary to make sure she hadn't gone native and thrown her lot in with the bad guys.

Our cover story, or 'legend', was as a new couple – we'd meet at the gym and take it from there. A nice easy way to slide me in for regular contacts, late nights and whispered phone calls. That being the case, it wouldn't do for us to be too familiar in case she gave the game away. The fact is that I don't like newbies. Don't trust them. Most of the times I've had things go wrong there's been a newbie involved and that just makes me suspicious of them. No matter how they turn out in the end, I need to get to understand them a little first. They also need to understand me; I make a point of not taking stick from anyone I don't have to and when things get nasty, I'm In Charge.

Hopefully the time for that conversation was a while off, and I had better things to be doing than contemplating my 'other half'. I wrote up a list of what I thought I'd need, based on the previous night's information, and emailed it across to Piers. There were a couple of special-order things on there, the sort we don't carry in stores, so the poor bugger would have to get a little exercise and do some shopping for me. I took a certain special joy in the fact that nobody else would have the clearance to arrange our supplies, so he wouldn't be able to palm it off on anyone else. I spent the rest of the day going over local maps and committing everything in the files to memory.

Day became night and another couple of awful ready meals went down my neck. The next morning, Piers delivered the kit with an expression that reminded me of a cat who'd just discovered that you'd taken a drunken dump in its litter tray last night. That brought the set-up phase to a conclusion and, having checked and packed everything carefully, I loaded the whole lot into the car and headed for the sticks.

I'd been set up with a flat on the outskirts of Bristol, within easy range of Annie's gym and a relatively painless commute to a nice dull job in town as some kind of computer consultant – someone else would do all the actual computer wrangling while I 'worked from home' a lot of the time. I'd lived in the flat, apparently, for about six months and it was all right – better than a lot of the holes I'd lived in as part of a cover, and definitely preferable to some of the observation posts I'd been half-buried in waiting for the right time to kill someone. One bedroom, bland decoration and no ornaments I'd have to fight the urge to destroy. My car this time was a silver Golf GTI, with standard plates that wouldn't show up as anything unusual with the local plod. I'd come across the locals once or twice before – the same force looks after Glastonbury, a breeding ground for loonies if ever there was one – and they had a patchy track record as far as I was concerned. Some of them were too bloody clever, and some wouldn't notice the sledgehammer in your hand if you were hitting them over the head with it. Fairly standard for cops, really. Getting my stuff in was a breeze: three bags in total, since I had a wardrobe already in place. Not quite me, but close enough. Too much stuff with labels for my taste, such as it is, but nice tailoring and nothing I wouldn't be able to fight in if I had to. Transferring weapons and other things that didn't fit the cover into the various safe holes around the flat, I started to get a sense of the place. I'd need to make it mine as quickly as possible, so I ordered a pizza and cracked a beer from the fridge. After all, that sort of rubbish would need to be in evidence to prove that this was a bachelor flat, and I'd eaten enough ready meals recently to be sick of the things.

It was Monday evening, which meant there was bugger all to do. I wasn't supposed to meet Annie until Thursday, so I had a few days to kill. My new job would suck some of that, obviously, but the rest was down to me so I decided to get on a bus, head into town and go to the pub. I found one just off the centre that was welcoming enough and sold decent beer, so I started the process of becoming a regular. By Wednesday night, they knew my name, what I did and what I like to drink, and they'd decided I was in. It was about all I could have done, and I didn't consider the time wasted. They even played blues music, which was nice, and I let them talk me into bringing my guitar down for the next open-mike night.

The day job seemed to be going all right as well. I was sliding into the company structure nicely, enjoying the attention from some of the girls in the call centre and not finding many of them particularly difficult to look at, either. One of the things I like about cover jobs is the feeling that no matter what you do, it's always 'no strings attached', even if it looks otherwise to everyone else. Once you've finished the op it's time to go, so you have a quick fling elsewhere, get dumped and move on, with whoever-she-was glad to see the back of you. Not particularly gallant, but if that's what you're looking for go read Malory.

So I had a flat, a job and a local. All I needed now was a girlfriend.

Thursday rolled round at last, and I headed to the gym. It was pricey, but my job was well paid enough to afford it and I was soon shunting weights in a room full of yuppies. Part of me was screaming in horror. This wasn't a gym, it was a singles bar – everyone was eyeing up everyone else with varying degrees of caution. But I had to admit that Annie looked pretty bloody impressive when she walked in – my earlier estimates of her attractions had clearly been somewhat short of the mark and the number of eyes following her across the room didn't exactly embarrass her. She spent some time on the weights, the rowing machine and the running thing that always strikes me as a complete waste of time. We managed to sort out a bit of eye contact as I did circuits, making sure that I was flexing like some kind of beauty show contestant but without bothering to put what I'd normally consider a full load on the bar – there was no sense in standing out, and I could have pressed twice what the yuppies were managing if I was in the right mood.

We managed to arrive at the juice bar within a couple of minutes of each other, did some more eye contact and then I moved in to chat her up. Nice and smooth. Phone numbers exchanged, plenty of flirting and we went our separate ways agreeing to meet on Saturday night, with me seriously wondering what she'd be like at other forms of exercise, since she wasn't exactly playing it virginal.

Saturday came in a blaze of sunlight and a mild hangover from a rock gig at my new local the previous evening. Much as I like a bit of loud music, the sight of a middle-aged beardy trying to belt out 'Paranoid' is enough to drive me to drink, and on this occasion I'd let it. The evening provided me with a good chance to get in with the landlord, though – a solid sort of bloke called Brian who used to be a bouncer and bought the place when he got lucky on the lottery. We had a couple of drinks after hours and talked about beer and ways to persuade drunks to leave, mixed with Brian's world-class collection of dirty jokes. He was even kind enough to let me know about a door job going in town, but I told him my regular gig was enough bollocks for one lifetime. I wasn't kidding about that; he just had a different frame of reference about what constituted my regular gig. I ended up rolling into a cab amidst a frenzy of lager louts and the women who (ahem) love them at two in the morning, looking somewhat tipsier than I actually was.

But the new day was ahead. I took a five-mile run to get a good look at my surroundings in a reasonably discreet fashion, fixed myself some brunch and meditated for a while to get my head in shape. No hangover in the world has withstood that little combination yet, so I was able to face the MI5 file with all guns blazing. It had arrived via encrypted email, and since my laptop was able to decrypt it on the fly there was no danger of it being written to the hard drive where some clever sod could find it. You try to plan for everything in this game, even if the odds on it happening are remote, and it wasn't entirely unlikely that my place might be searched once the Sisters thought I was intimate with one of their own.

The file was dull, but added a little depth to what I already knew. More about Hamilton's politics and associates at university, where she'd hung out with some obvious bad 'uns judging by the number of cross-references. There was also an interesting sideline about an affair with a woman from the US Air Force, who'd been shipped home and drummed out the moment it became known that she was spending time with the enemy. I'd have to track that one down at some point, see what happened to her. Apart from that, we already knew more about Hamilton than she did herself – we'd grabbed her DNA from when she donated blood a couple of years back, and her fingerprints from the cutlery in a vegetarian café she liked; the CCTV cameras now all over Britain gave us as many pictures of her as we could have possibly desired. She lived and breathed at our discretion – literally – and the only secrets she had were those she worked bloody hard to protect. With Annie in the picture, even those were starting to become ours. Just like we know every other citizen, we knew everything that could be known about Sadie Hamilton and were working on the rest.

I'd chosen a quiet little restaurant in town for my date with Annie, something classy without being too expensive, to supposedly impress her with my good taste and give a signal to anyone watching that I was just a regular bloke trying to get into her knickers. Soft music and candlelight aided the illusion and we spent an evening talking about inconsequential things. After all, there was no point going to all that trouble and then screwing up on something as elementary as eavesdropping. Annie turned out to be pleasant company – funny, clever, just a tiny bit flirty and sexy as hell. She'd picked out a little black dress that hugged in all the best places and stopped at just the right height to let you glimpse a hint of stocking top when she moved a certain way. Once she'd moved that way a couple of times it was easy enough to forget that this was work and just settle into the evening. Unlike a lot of what I do, this was a genuinely pleasant date; most of the time I work with people I wouldn't touch with somebody else's, or with other blokes, and sharing dinner with a beautiful woman reminded me of the civilian world where you're not risking death every time you go to work and your home phone number isn't a bloody state secret. Yet again, I thought about quitting, but knew the same as always that it would never be an option.

We finished the evening with drinks at a vodka bar, her brushing up against me in a way that felt real and my hand wandering around her waist and nearby environs. When the taxi delivered us to her place, I got the most incredible snog – but no more. I headed back into the cab with a look of disappointment, and the taxi driver commiserated with me all the way home.

Exactly as planned.

We'd already decided that she wasn't going to put out until the second date; we figured that was as keen as she could be and still hold on to some respect among the Sisterhood for keeping me around. Shag me and forget was fine, it seemed, but if I was to be longer term then I had to work for it a little. No problem. In fact, if that evening was anything to go by I thought I was going to enjoy dating Annie.

Chapter Three

Karen Thomas lived in a terraced house in a moderately pleasant suburb on the northern edge of Bristol; a nice, respectable home for a nice, respectable member of the community. Her neighbours wouldn't have known anything about what happened at her 'Women's Group' meetings, that was for sure. Anyone in a position of responsibility around kids would have to keep that quiet or the tabloids would be after them like hounds after a fox, a situation we'd engineered during the sixties and one the media were happy to cooperate with in the interests of a story. The British press is a wonderful thing to someone like me; it allows reputations to be destroyed in an instant and voices that would otherwise cause all sorts of problems to be ignored behind cries of 'Pervert!' For an open-minded, cross-cultural society, we Brits do a splendid job of acting like uptight maiden aunts sometimes.

The garden was walled, which gave me a good working area without too much danger of observation. Annie had told me that a meeting was on that night and, as a member of the inner circle, Karen would need to be there. It was the perfect opportunity to arrange Annie's promotion.

Two locks, both mortise type. No need to worry about holding anything open, then – just a matter of shifting the bolts open on the way in and closing them on the way out. Easy. I pulled my picks out and got to work. There are gadgets now that you just stick in the lock and they make all the effort, but I'm not a fan. They can leave scratches that a good forensic tech will spot as being out of place, and that makes me nervous. I'm an old-fashioned sort of boy who believes that 'leave no trace' means exactly that and if that means I have to sit out in the open for another thirty seconds, then it's a risk I'll calculate. Tonight, that risk was justified: I had good cover, low light and no guarantee that any traces I left wouldn't make it back to Hamilton and her crew. I'd already taken as many precautions as I could before I left – a cleansing bath in salt water with protective oils and a meditation that was still running in a small part of the back of my mind to mask my psychic signature and let me pass through the house without leaving any traces on that level. Stealth in this business isn't just about a cool ninja suit and being able to creep around in the shadows – magicians have more options for finding and spotting people, so 'careful' is a word that doesn't even begin to describe the kind of preparations you need to get away with this kind of thing.

In less than a minute, I had both locks open. I slipped an interrupter between the alarm contacts on the door, moved inside and headed straight for the alarm box in the front hall. A few seconds with a black box from the geeks back home and that was sorted. My night-vision goggles gave me a great view of the place without the need for a torch or anything else that would attract attention, so I started looking for the study. Sure enough, it looked as if everything I wanted was together in the spare bedroom. I fired up Karen's computer, attached the second gadget

I was carrying and let that empty her computer of everything it knew. At the same time I was working through her paper files, looking for the inevitable Book of Shadows – a witch's notebook of work done, spells and various other things of use. It wasn't in the filing cabinet or the desk, so I stepped into the bedroom and had a quick check through the chest of drawers. Bingo – in with her underwear, which was surprisingly racy in some parts. I didn't have her down for transparent mesh, but you never can tell with some people and she was already hiding one aspect of her life. Not bothering to suppress my grin, I started photographing the book page by page. It looked like it was in some form of code, but the boys back home would deal with that – any code that can be held in the mind well enough to write in like a language is effectively just another language, which means that it can be cracked with enough computer time. Not my problem, anyway; I'd send the data upstairs, and get the results back. You can't be good at everything, after all, and I doubt that any of our crypto boys would be much use in my shoes.

The underwear had given me hope for the next phase of the job. Having finished with the book and replaced it exactly where I found it, I started checking the bedside table. Here there were many more joys: a set of restraints, some candles and a selection of dildos – one of which was the size of a police baton. Something that size meant I was going to find what I was hoping for: lubricant.

Karen had a selection of flavours, but strawberry seemed to be favourite judging by the amount left in the bottle. Strangely enough, this one actually smelled of strawberries, so I made a mental note of the brand as I pulled out a capsule of colourless liquid and added it to the bottle. I dosed the unflavoured lube as well, just to be sure, since that also seemed to have had a fair amount of use. Again replacing everything exactly as it had been, I gave the room a final going over just to be sure. Apart from a couple of very compromising photos that explained the equipment in the bedside cabinet (of which I snapped copies) there was nothing else of interest. Karen was reasonably careful. Unfortunately for her, I am at times a deeply *un*reasonable man.

Collecting the data thingy from the study, which had already closed down the computer after wiping any traces of its presence, I checked over the rest of the house. Nothing useful I could find in the time. If the chance presented itself, we could always have someone else check the place after the main job was complete. Considering the evening's work as done as possible, I reset the alarm, locked the door behind me and made my way back to the car, which was parked a few streets away.

The decrypts came back only a day later. Whatever code she'd used (there were notes, but they were too technical for me) was sufficiently close to established techniques that the boffins didn't even have to make much of an effort. The first thing that struck me was the difference between the outer and inner circles; the inner was very fond of sex and drugs, which explained what I had found at Karen's house. Serious mind-bending stuff, judging from what she'd written – shamanic journeys and lots of altered states of consciousness. What struck me most, though, was where they were trying to go. A normal journey would involve heading off into the Netherworld, getting some information and heading back to share it with the rest of the world. In this case, they were looking for *someone*. The notes didn't make it clear who they were after, so I assumed it was going to be someone sufficiently interesting to make writing the name potentially dangerous. That didn't leave many options – a couple of the Elder Gods, some demons and a few dead mages who were looking for a way back. I made a note to check with the divination boys and ask them to see if anything was unusually active on the Other Side. The rest of it was concerned with the reactions that Karen had had to the work. She'd obviously lightened up in her private life, judging by the entries over time; there was a fair element of sex diary there and her trips to London had involved a few clubs I knew, mainly on the fetish scene. Once Hamilton had got Karen to open Pandora's box, Karen had developed a taste for increasingly extreme experiences – the more intense the better. That might come in useful later, as I had friends in the scene who owed me a few favours.

Her computer offered more evidence of this. She belonged to a couple of online dating services, and she'd been active on a few newsgroups specialising in hard BDSM, body piercing and tattoos, most likely investigating before taking another step along her path. Sensible girl. The worlds of fetish and magic don't cross over that much, but when they do it tends to be a quest for intensity. I remember a girl I used to know who was fond of cuffs but could be made to hold perfectly still and orgasm just by modulating the energy in my voice, let alone what could happen with contact, so that didn't worry me particularly. Karen had been discreet, and played responsibly; the rules here were the fetish scene's standards: safe, sane and consensual. What struck me about the whole thing was the fact that she hadn't started unwinding until she joined the inner circle. Up until that point, she seemed to have been pretty mundane but whatever had happened during her initiation had set her loose at quite a rate. Two years later, she was apparently prepared to consider doing almost anything with almost anyone – if you floated her boat and the circumstances were right it was a sure thing.

I started to worry a little about Annie. I decided to warn her about what I'd found the next time I saw her.

Wednesday night saw me back at the pub with a guitar in my lap, singing the blues to a group of enthusiastic amateur musicians and their friends. Having heard the competition the previous week, and since most of the same faces were there again, I decided to go with something soft and melancholy for my introduction – a cover of 'The Thrill is Gone'. Since this went down well enough to stop much of the background chatter, I moved on to a couple of others, finishing with a version of 'How Blue Can You Get' that had everyone laughing in all the right places and applauding at the end. The free pint that earned me tasted fantastic and Mike, the youngish bloke who organised the night for Brian, insisted that I come back and play again. I even ended up accompanying a girl who was singing, and the combination of her voice and my guitar silenced the whole room for three full minutes. Stuff all the messing around with pentagrams, that was *real* magic.

It was good to be doing something normal for a change. The day job was starting to bore me and the on/off nature of being back-up man to Annie really wasn't my idea of a good time. I prefer short, sharp hits, or being on the inside myself. But for those few minutes of music, I could be Jack again; just a man playing his guitar and weeping for the world through his music. So what if it's pretentious, it makes me happy.

Saturday rolled round with another hangover – Brian had dragged me out to another pub for a few beers and to introduce me to some of his mates. Splendid beer, but perhaps a little too much; this time I was almost as drunk as I looked when I rolled into the taxi home, but didn't regret an instant of it. I'd judged the intake level carefully, so I could keep the story straight and one eye on what was happening around me. Even though I knew it was only a cover, a night out like that is the closest thing there is to having a life while I'm on the job. I did the same run and meditate combination as before, took a nice long bath and got my act together for date number two with Annie.

This time it was a Chinese restaurant in a suburb conveniently close to my place. While the food was all right, the place was discreet enough to let us play a little footsie under the table and enjoy a fair number of meaningful glances over it. Anyone watching would have had no doubt that we'd be sharing a cab home, that's for sure – and that's exactly what we did.

We rolled through the front door of my flat in the middle of another one of Annie's incredible kisses. That girl certainly had quite a talent with her tongue, and it was a wrench to get back to business once I'd kicked the door shut behind us. I'd left my laptop in the bedroom, and the portable hard drive with all the useful data was in a hiding place within easy reach of the bed, so I picked Annie up and carried her into the bedroom – making a nice silhouette on the curtains for anyone who might have been outside. She squealed prettily as I threw her down on the bed, so I whispered in her ear, 'How much foreplay would you like?'

She grinned. 'Ooh, loads – I wish every man asked me that!' With that, she stretched out and moaned softly, then sat up and switched on my laptop as I connected the drive. She kept making the noises as she read, and I pointed out the more important bits as we came to them. She seemed intrigued by Karen's awakening, but not worried. By the time she'd got about halfway through that she put the laptop to one side and faked an orgasm that would have probably got me a reference as a good shag from the neighbours. Picking up the laptop again, she started moving her hips to rock the bed as she read. I joined in with the rhythm, slow at first, and soon we had an authentic-sounding noise of headboard meeting wall. We varied the speed a few times and once Annie had finished reading Karen's Book of Shadows, she moved things up a notch and let go another screamer. Figuring it was only polite, I joined in with a few grunts of my own and had a nice loud moan at the end.

I ditched my shirt, shoes, socks and trousers, then threw on a robe. 'Coffee?'

'Mmm, please,' Annie replied. 'You've quite taken it out of me for the moment. Was it good for you?'

'Well, I feel like a cigarette, if that helps.'

I headed into the kitchen and fixed us a pot. Then I put the stereo on to cover our 'pillow talk' and headed back. Annie was reading Karen's newsgroup posts with an expression of intense interest.

'This is a side we never saw at the meetings – she always seemed so uptight.'

'You should have seen her bedroom. All sorts of fun toys, and I'd love to know what she was wearing under those suits when you saw her.' I gave her an idea of Karen's tastes in lingerie, enjoying the sight of Annie's eyebrows climbing when I got to the knickers that came with a built-in butt plug. 'Maybe she did have a stick up her ass after all.'

'I'd never have guessed!'

'That's the point. It's obvious that what happens on the inside isn't like what you've been doing so far. You hang on to your marbles in there, OK?'

'Sure thing, Bill. I can take care of myself.'

'Of course you can. But don't let things go too far too quickly. These people are obviously heavy on the consciousness-altering shit and you need to keep a handle on who you are as well as who you're supposed to be. Don't pretend it's easy, because that can lead you into trouble. You get me?'

'Yes, Bill, I get you. Now how about another one?' She waggled her eyebrows at me.

'What the hell, I'm a fit lad.' I started moving the bed again and she joined in with me straight away. Listening to her moans, I found myself getting quite hot under the collar, and she seemed to be enjoying herself as well. But no nookie for us. It doesn't do to shag the help.

The next morning I went out and grabbed a paper as Annie showered. I found what I was looking for on page three – 'Local Teacher Dies in Bed'. According to the report, Karen Thomas, a 32-year-old woman who taught at St Benedict's School, was found dead on Saturday afternoon by a friend who was concerned about milk left outside and curtains still drawn when they'd agreed to meet at lunchtime. Cause of death was believed to be a heart attack, and the police were not treating it as suspicious.

I showed it to Annie, who seemed surprised. I think, for a moment, that she managed to convince herself it was a coincidence. Once that attempt failed, she shot back to the bathroom and emptied her stomach. I wandered after her.

'Now that's sorted, you can move into her position.'

'But how? You were with me all night. When did you . . . ?'

'Monday. It just took her this long to get round to making contact with the toxin.'

'What did you do, exactly?'

'I introduced a chemical into her bloodstream that would normally raise her heartbeat to a dangerous level. Since it would have been ingested while her heart rate was already elevated, it would have sent her system over the edge. Poor woman, bad heart.'

'Nothing to link it to us, then?'

'Of course not.' I managed not to look offended. 'I'm

a professional, Annie. Leave No Trace, remember?'

'Did you have to kill her?'

'What did you expect me to do, pack her off to the Bahamas for a fortnight? They'd do exactly the same thing to us if they knew who we were, and the sooner you get your head around that the better. This game is played for keeps, Annie. Always was, always will be. They kill us, we kill them, and nobody knows a bloody thing about it. Now sort your shit out and look pretty for the outside world – there's still a chance we're being watched.'

I left her in the bathroom to wash her face, brush her teeth and check that she hadn't got vomit anywhere on her. By the time she re-emerged everything was back in place. Maybe she would work out after all. The first kill's never easy, and she obviously understood that she'd killed Karen Thomas with a couple of words back at the flat in Chelsea. Once I'd dropped her off at home, I returned to my place and finished the paper. I love regional newspapers, they're so civilised. Once somebody blabbed to the tabloids, they'd be all over this like a rash. I'd only put the poison in two places and, since it only took a few minutes to soak into the bloodstream and do its job, I had a bloody good idea about what Karen Thomas had been doing when she died.

Chapter Four

Annie and I now had a reason to see each other more regularly – good sex. While cover jobs, her coven and my music got in the way, we figured that we'd be able to see each other twice a week at least without it causing any suspicion. She'd had to go to Karen's funeral, of course – a fine, upstanding Christian ceremony that matched her life in the outside world. The following weekend, however, the coven had held its own mourning ceremony for their lost sister and, just as planned, Annie had been invited to join the inner circle.

'It was quite a show,' she told me in bed after another successful Wednesday-night gig and hour or so's fakery. 'Twice as many candles and everyone in black robes, with one laid out on the floor for Karen. We sang sad songs for her and sent her on her way, then the outer circle was dismissed except for me and I was offered Karen's robe to wear in place of my own. Wherever she is, I bet that pissed her off.' I had my own ideas about where Karen had ended up, but hadn't arranged anything special so wasn't in a position to make any accurate guesses. Annie kept talking. 'One thing, though. They say I have to get Karen's permission to take her place before I can be fully initiated. Isn't that going to, you know, blow the game?'

'Don't worry,' I said, 'I'll take care of it.'

'How?'

'Don't ask.' Better she didn't know, actually. If she realised how far I was going to have to go to keep her safe she'd probably have been sick all over the toilet again, and I didn't fancy clearing it up. 'When's the ceremony?'

'Sunday night.'

'No problem.'

'Oh.' She looked thoughtfully at me for a second as I lay there putting a plan together. 'Did you really have to kill her? Couldn't you just have, I don't know, made her disappear or something?'

'I wish I could have, Annie, but I had a feeling something like this might happen and if she's not there when you go looking, Hamilton will know something's up. Then you'd be in trouble.'

'I suppose so, Bill, but it just gets me that the only way to solve a problem is to kill the person concerned. Can't we just scare them out of whatever they've got planned?'

'No, we can't. This isn't some dodgy antique dealer we can just lean on, Annie, these are terrorists. They've got a history of acting against the state, of trying to mess with people's lives and of doing some fairly nasty things to people's heads. Think about Karen for a second. Two years ago she was an ordinary schoolteacher with an interest in Wicca, but she died a revolutionary who hated everything her life stood for. I'm all for personal growth, but that smacks of mind control.'

'I guess—'

'Well, I know. I've been doing this a lot longer than you, and I've seen it before. All we can do is stop them, and prevent the spread of their ideas and techniques.

This isn't about a couple of dozen women who want to change the world peacefully, this is about eight terrorists up to no good. Remember the oath you took when you joined up?'

'Vaguely. Something about defending the people from stuff.'

'It's called the Defence of the Realm. It's what we're here for. It's about making sure little Johnny down the road can sleep safely without the monsters coming out of his closet and eating him. It's about letting people follow their spiritual paths without someone else hijacking their souls. It's about letting everyone believe what they want to. The alternatives are chaos or witch-hunters, and while I can't say I like the way we do things, it sucks a lot less than the other two options.'

'Yeah, I know. Doesn't mean I have to like it, though.'

'Hold on to that, Annie. When you start liking what we do, that's the time to worry.'

We both headed off to our jobs in the morning, but I was worried about Annie. It struck me that she was experiencing some kind of crisis about the job, and at just the wrong time. I knew that Karen had basically been a victim, but that didn't make me regret my actions. When you're dealing with this sort of disease, radical surgery is the only answer – no different from cutting off an infected limb to save the body. I wasn't kidding about the alternatives, either; the only other way to control this would be a return to the days of the Witchfinder General and the hysteria and needless bloodshed that went with it. Our way – identifying rogue elements and eliminating them while allowing others to continue on safer paths – is as clean as it can get. I just had to be sure that Annie understood that, since wavering now could land her in some pretty nasty trouble.

We saw each other again on Friday, and Annie seemed better, though still a little subdued. I got the impression she'd been doing some thinking about things, and had managed to get a grip on the war we were fighting. I didn't like having to rip away what was left of her innocence like that, but I really didn't have a choice. She gave me as much information about Sunday's meeting as possible, but since she'd not been told much – just where and when to meet the others – it wasn't much help. I was still going to have to do the hard part, but at least she had the good sense not to ask me about it this time.

Sunday afternoon rolled round far too quickly for my liking. I'd had time to quietly assemble all the kit I'd need, including a deserted cottage out in the middle of nowhere for the actual operation. I threw everything I needed from the flat into a bag and went to find a large silver-backed mirror. That last item came from an antique shop in Gloucester, which was as far as I could travel if I was going to get the job done in time.

Sunset found me in the aforementioned cottage, out in the Cotswolds and miles from anywhere. I'd set up in what looked as if it used to be the main sitting room, which was large enough for the job and still had a roof to protect me from the weather. I'd cleared out the remnants of teenage drinking and swept the place thoroughly before marking as big a pentagram as I could in salt on the floor. The mirror went on its stand at the western edge, with a candle to either side, and the other candles marked the necessary points around the edge of the circle. I set incense burning in a couple of bowls, checked that everything I'd need was inside the circle and stripped off. Then it was time to clear my mind and begin.

With an incantation I knew by heart (mainly because it was part of advanced survival training) I sealed the circle. Nothing supernatural was going to cross that line now until I did, and anything else would now feel like avoiding the place until I was done. I was taking a big risk with this ritual in more ways than one and I really didn't want to chance being disturbed. Luckily for me, the people I especially didn't want to notice would be busy with their own preparations at that point.

Next came the devotions, then the set-up. Once I knew I was ready, I started with the Latin. I was using the nasty book again, which generally puts the willies up me before and after, but nothing was going to keep Annie alive tonight except good old-fashioned Black Magic and Annie was my priority. She was a good kid, and was starting to show that she might just have the stones to do the job. If she got through this well, I might not mention the wobble she'd had earlier. No point screwing her career over one minor mistake.

Once I'd finished the incantation, it was time to summon Karen. Calling her name and reciting the charm of summoning, I watched the mirror as my reflection faded and hers started to appear. Funnily enough, she didn't look happy to see me; but the way

I'd set the enchantments meant she had no choice about being there – she was trapped until I released her.

Then it was time for the really dangerous bit. In the same way that the dead can possess the living, I was going to possess one of the dead. With another turn of Latin, I reached out to the mirror as Karen, powerless to resist, did the same. My fingers froze to the surface as I touched the glass, and my body went rigid. I'd be standing there until the end, now. In the mirror, Karen looked frightened as she realised what I was doing – something she obviously hadn't thought possible up until then. As I stared into the mirror, her eyes grew larger and larger until . . .

I was standing on a plain, looking through the mirror at my body standing rigid in the cottage. A cold wind blew around me, chilling me to the bone as I looked down and saw Karen's body. I tried moving, getting used to the lack of pulse and breathing – that stuff was still happening back in the Cotswolds. Then I set off across the plain, marking my starting position carefully so I could get home once I'd finished. Great winged *things* flew overhead, and the wind blew constantly without any variation. Other spirits moved around the place, looking lost and frightened – obviously the recently dead trying to come to terms with what had happened to them before going on to wherever they were planning to go. I could feel Karen deep inside the back of my head, screaming and railing to be released. She had to warn her sisters that something was wrong and that was what was keeping her there, a task I'd specifically come to prevent her completing. Out there, the dead can tell any number of tales if they're sufficiently motivated and while she didn't know who was responsible, she was quite keenly aware that her death had not been as natural as it had appeared.

While I was waiting for the summons from Hamilton and her group, I ran through what Karen had written about her own initiation to be sure of what to do when the time came. Karen was still trying to fight me, but since I'd broken her will to get inside her, there wasn't much she could do to stop me any more. I pushed her back far enough to cut out most of the sound of her screams, but not so far that I wouldn't hear her respond to the summons.

It felt as if I'd been there a week when the call came, somewhere between a whisper in my ear and a shout in the distance. I turned and walked towards it, feeling Karen desperately fighting for enough control at least to stop me from going there if not to regain complete control of her body. I forced her back again, making my way straight towards a depression in the landscape.

Nine women were standing in a circle, all naked. They were chanting in Old English, not unlike a group of nuns, with calls from Hamilton to which the others responded. I could see Annie, looking terrified opposite Hamilton, joining in the responses with less confidence than the others. I entered their circle, knowing that I wouldn't be able to leave it without their permission but trusting my acting skills to get me the hell out of there. Hamilton looked me in the eye and smiled.

'Welcome, sister, we greet you one last time.'

I raised my hand, just as Karen remembered.

'We come before you with the one we would have take your place in our circle, now that you have stepped beyond the veil of death.' Hamilton pointed behind me to Annie, and I turned to face her. 'Will you surrender your place to her? Will you trust her to serve as loyally as you have? Look into her heart and see her in truth. Is she one of us?'

I stepped forward to look at Annie. I could see her terror as only the dead can. I saw her seeming loyalty to the group and her true loyalty to the Service. That she was repulsed by me back in the world, but couldn't help an attraction. I felt Karen try to scream a denouncement and crushed it in an instant. I turned back to Hamilton and spoke my lines.

'This woman is my sister as she is yours. I give my place to her, for she will serve loyally with all her heart. She is worthy to know our secrets, for she will keep them safe.' With that I turned to Annie, who was doing a magnificent job of hiding the shock this response caused her, and embraced her.

'We thank you, sister,' Hamilton said behind me. 'Go now in peace, and find your reward.' I turned back to her, bowed and left the circle the way I had come as the women shimmered out of existence behind me.

All the way back to the mirror I could feel Karen wailing. She'd failed in her last duty to the Sisterhood, that of protecting them from traitors joining the inner circle. I couldn't let myself feel sympathy for her, not yet. I had to get back to my body before dawn, and preferably before anything discovered the gate I'd opened between that place and the outside world. I didn't expect to be in a fit state for an exorcism after this.

But we were good. The mirror was where I'd left it, with my body on the other side. I assumed a position that reflected my own, reached out and touched the surface. Warmth flooded back into my body as I returned to the land of the living and I shuddered as my mind remembered how to breathe, pump blood and digest food. It wasn't much of a surprise to discover that I was ravenously hungry.

Looking into the mirror, I could see Karen still trapped there. She was wailing again, but that didn't come as much of a surprise. Only one thing left to do now, and I could go. Reading a last passage from the book, I stood to one side of the mirror, away from the edge of the circle, and brought a small silver hammer round to crack the glass. There was an enormous bang as the entire mirror crumbled to powder, shot out across the circle and swirled around the edge, finally settling in a circle on top of the salt I'd used to mark the floor.

Karen wasn't going anywhere now. I'd effectively destroyed her immortal soul.

It took me an hour to clear up, collecting all the powdered glass and salt with a battery-powered vacuum cleaner and returning the rest of my gear to the holdall I'd brought it in. I dropped the residue into the first river I came across, scattering it in such a way that no one would ever be able to contact Karen again, nor would she be able to get a warning through to the others. If anybody wanted her now they'd have to find all the remnants of the mirror, down to the very last speck of glass dust. Then I went straight home, called in sick to the office and slept until Wednesday morning.

Chapter Five

I had to wait until Wednesday night before I saw Annie again anyway, and I needed the sleep after what I'd pulled with Karen. I played another gig at the jam night, some Robert Johnson this time (slow and mournful seemed fitting), and a couple of guys had approached me about forming a band with them. I'd told them that it sounded like fun and to get back to me about it, because I rather liked the idea despite knowing it was pointless. I was going to be gone in a couple of months, and the extra attention was potentially dangerous. The jam night had been a bit of a stretch, but I was sick of being stuck with session work between assignments and had never lost the love of playing for an audience of actual people rather than just the studio techs. Not only that, it was nice to be liked by people for a change. I see so much fear and suffering that a happy room where I'm participating is good for me. Annie had come to listen, of course, and we'd got out of there as quickly as we could for what people thought was the obvious reason.

After an hour and a half of the standard headboard banging, we were able to get down to business. Annie was clearly frightened by what she wanted to tell me, so I had to start her off, but once she got going, she seemed happy to be able to tell someone else.

'You were right. They are terrorists.' I nodded but said nothing. 'Once we'd finished the ritual to talk to Karen they had no problem opening up to me. What the hell happened there, anyway?'

'Don't ask. But tell me what happened with that later – I'd be interested to know what you saw.'

'Hmm. Well, they're working with another group, mostly male from the way Sadie talks about them, and they're planning something big. Something political. I think it's supposed to be the start of something bigger, but the start's big enough.'

'And that is?'

'They're going to kill the Prime Minister.'

I was speechless for a second. I knew they were bad news, but this was out of their league without help; that would explain the other group, who were probably the more traditional type of terrorist outfit.

'The PM? Oh, for fuck's sake.'

'Preparations have already started, which is why they wanted someone to replace Karen quickly. It's scheduled for the next full moon.' Annie was looking more agitated now, and I didn't blame her. This was more serious than either of us had been expecting.

'Just over three weeks away.'

'We'll go underground a week or so before the hit, to give us time to set the ritual up. I'm scared, Bill – what happens if it works?'

'It won't. Now we know the plan, we can have them rounded up and dealt with. Besides, they're not going to be able to manage anything with you on the inside, are they? They need the whole circle to be willing for it to work, and you're not about to kill the head of Her Majesty's Government, are you?'

'Well, no. But seriously, you're going to have them picked up?'

'Of course I am. This'll all be over soon, and we can go home. When's the next meeting?'

'Tomorrow night. That's when I'll get the rest of the briefing.'

'OK. Then you'll go to that, get what you can and come here to report on Friday. We'll grab them over the weekend. Are you going to be all right with that?'

Annie smiled. 'Sure. In, out, report. Then we're done?'

'Then we're done.'

'So what did happen with Karen?'

'A little something to make her cooperate with us for a while.'

'Oh. She's . . . all right, isn't she?'

'No one will ever hurt her again. She's gone to another place.'

'Good. I feel sorry for her, y'know?'

'I know. But it's all over for her now.'

I got Annie to tell me the tale from her point of view. It had been a fairly standard summoning ritual, with the eight original members calling for their lost sister, then the initiate joining in with the welcome when they knew Karen was on the way. Annie made no bones about being frightened by the consequences of Karen telling tales, as she'd been told that any sign of disloyalty would be quickly discovered and punished with the same speed by Karen possessing her body and retaking her place among the nine. It was possible, of course, but I doubted Hamilton could have done it on the spot. That's some fairly potent magic, but then so was the ritual I'd performed.

I decided to take the leap and tell her what I'd done. She was understandably stunned.

'You possessed her? I thought it only worked the other way round?'

'Depends on what you've got to play with. That little trick came from an old sixteenth-century manuscript we pulled out of circulation years ago. It's one of the things we keep to ourselves, stuff that lets us work under the radar. If everybody knew about it, the Sisterhood wouldn't have accepted you like they did.'

'I guess so. But what about Karen? Did she suffer?'

'Not at all.' I was lying through my teeth at that point, but it was what Annie needed to hear. Karen had suffered and screamed every second since I first called her, and if anyone managed to put that mirror back together and pull her out of it she'd be screaming still.

'And after?'

'I moved her on. She's somewhere else, where no one can reach her. You're safe, and she's gone.'

Annie fell asleep shortly after that, but I stayed up long enough to encode a report and send it off to the Boss. The Head Shed needed to know about this double-quick, and they'd want a couple of days to assemble a team that could get all eight targets in one night. What we really wanted, though, was the name of the other group. If we only got half the beast, it could still bite.

An answer from the Boss came back the following day. I wasn't able to pick it up until after work and the near-obligatory pint, but that wasn't especially important since there was nothing I could do about it until I saw Annie.

Pick-up teams being prepared. Collect all possible information before activation of roll-up plan. NF371 [Annie's identification code for the job] *to remain with group until all possible information has been extracted. Strongly suggest you do not act until last possible moment to facilitate capture of secondary group. Well done. Zero.* ///*Ends*

It was the closest thing to a compliment the Boss ever gave ('Zero' was his personal ID code) and the closest thing he could to an order. On a job like this, the field officer is in charge. Normally, that would be Annie because she was actually in the group, but since she was also as green as the grass at Lord's I'd been assigned command when I joined in. It was felt, quite accurately, that Annie would have trouble with this phase: the part when all her friends, all the people who'd trusted her for over a year and a half and whose lives she'd shared, would be picked up in the middle of the night and never seen by the outside world again. The Boss knew I wouldn't give a toss, but he wanted me to hang Annie out for as long as possible to get all the information she could about the other group. It stank, but I had to agree with him.

Later that night, as I was reviewing likely candidates for the other half of the hit, the door buzzer rang. Tying up my bathrobe and reaching for an extending baton, I hit the CCTV feed for the front door. There was a spy hole, but whoever's on the other side can see when you're looking through at them and that's just asking to get shot.

Annie was outside. She was wrapped in an overcoat and looked harassed and out of breath. Her hair was tousled and her cheeks flushed. Since she wasn't supposed to be anywhere near me until Friday night, something must have gone wrong. There were no alternatives; I'd have to hide her until we could get the two of us out safely.

As I opened the door, Annie pushed through it, grabbing my face and locking her lips on mine. The kiss was more intense than anything we'd faked previously – hungrier, more desperate. She kicked the door closed behind her and looked me in the eye, breathing hard.

'Christ,' she said, 'I don't know what was in the sacrament tonight, but it's left me feeling *seriously* horny.'

'OK, Annie. Try to keep your head. I'll see what I've got to bring you down.'

'Nooo!' she wailed as I tried to pull away. 'I know what I need, I just need your help to get it.' With that, she grabbed my hands and moved them to her thighs, sliding them up towards her waist. I could feel her stockings and suspenders as the skirt rode up with her hands. She curled a leg around mine and kissed me again.

'Annie, keep it together. You can do it. Just remember you don't have to do this.'

'But I want to.' She undid my robe, pulled it off and started kissing my chest. I pushed her away and she landed on the sofa. 'Oh yeah, I like it a bit rough!'

'Jesus, Annie. Stop this!' While my mind was staying professional, another part of me had other ideas entirely. Annie noticed, licked her lips, shed her coat and started to crawl towards me on all fours, her skirt now all the way up around her waist, exposing a sight I'd normally find thoroughly enjoyable.

'Oh, come on, Bill, you can't tell me you don't want to. I've seen the way you look at me. Why not see it all?' She got up on her knees, pulling the dress over her head to reveal what little she had on underneath – a black silk suspender belt and thong. Me being stark naked with a raging hard-on didn't exactly help matters for either of us. As she started moving forward I backed up to keep the distance between us. Then the armchair hit me in the back of my knees and I found myself sitting down. That was all the invitation she needed. She almost leapt across the room to me and found another way to show me what an incredible kisser she was.

At that point, frankly, I lost it. I grabbed her hair, pulled her up to me and kissed her hard. She moaned with pleasure and stuck her tongue far enough down the back of my throat to see what I'd had for dinner, then wrapped her legs round my waist and my big head stopped doing the thinking. She was even louder than when she'd been faking it, with a mouth as dirty as the things she wanted to do. At some point we ended up in the bedroom, because after she'd got whatever it was out of her system, we lay on the bed and talked about what the Sisterhood were up to.

'The other outfit's called Eleven-Eleven,' she told me, 'radical anarchists who've managed to get guns and money from somewhere and are looking for an excuse to use them. Sadie seems to know the leader from way back. She says this is the best way to start tearing down the established structures of male dominance and put women back in charge where they should be.'

'Same old feminist bollocks, then.'

'"Same old feminist bollocks"! Well, isn't that just like a man? All you want to do is fuck and kill. No creativity, just destruction.' I didn't like the sound of that, but I was too tired to argue and didn't really want to interrupt her flow.

'Whatever. Any idea how they're going to do it?'

'Something to do with the weather. We've been practising making it rain.'

I looked out of the window – it was pissing down. 'Going well, then, is it?'

'Hell yeah, and they're big on sex magic, too. We were daisy-chained right round the pentagram bringing this storm on.' Lightning flashed outside.

'Maybe that's why you're so—'

'Turned on? Horny? Who cares?'

I looked her in the eyes, deathly serious. 'Annie, I think you should stay here for a couple of days. Something's not right and I think you need a break.'

'I'm fine.' She looked down with a gleam in her eye. 'And so are you. Looks like a break was just what you needed.' With that she leapt on me again and shagged me till I passed out from exhaustion.

The next morning I was awake before her, coding up a report while the coffee brewed. I'd just sent it off when I heard a shriek from the bedroom. Annie was awake and remembering what had happened. I arrived at the doorway to see her looking at the state of the bed and her own sore body. It had been a rough night, at her insistence, and she was obviously feeling it. She looked up at me dressed in a bathrobe and blanched.

'Oh Jesus fuck, what have I done?' she asked, mostly to herself. Then, sobbing, she got off the bed, pushed past me into the living room, grabbed her coat and shoes and was through the front door before I could stop her, leaving the rest of her clothes where they'd been thrown the previous night.

Chapter Six

I let Annie go, figuring she'd be a little more compos mentis once she'd had time to calm down. Not only that, but I was still trying to figure out what had happened. I'm normally more in control than that and, while Annie was good, I should have been able to hold myself back far more effectively. An idea struck me, and I went straight to my medical kit. The kit was somewhat better supplied than a normal one for the home, with sutures, serious painkillers, splints, plaster of Paris and what I was looking for – a syringe. I needed a blood sample, and mine would have to do in place of Annie's.

Having called the cover office and told them I'd be working from home, I threw some clothes on and drove straight to Annie's. Her car wasn't outside, and she wasn't answering the door, so I let myself in with the spare key she'd given me for emergencies. The place was a mess, as though she'd not tidied in a week. Washing-up was piled in the sink, and scattered around the front room were books on various types of magic and Goddess worship and a fair amount of radical feminist literature of the 'cut off their dicks and keep 'em in cages' sort. Judging from the way pages had been folded back and parts underlined, they'd seen a fair amount of use. Was this research, or something else? It was difficult to say, so I explored further.

The bedroom was as untidy as the rest of the place, and the sheets bore stains similar to the ones back at my place. She'd obviously been a busy girl that week. A small collection of sex toys lay under one pillow, within easy reach. It seemed that Annie's libido had been on the rise and she'd been trying to keep it under control. At least her underwear hadn't suddenly turned into leather and PVC; all the stuff I'd got used to seeing was still there, although she had a few more silk and satin things than I'd been allowed to get near. It was clear enough that she hadn't been back there that day, though, so I tried ringing her cellphone. I left a message on her voicemail, with a nice calm voice so she'd not think I was angry with her, then tried her office number. She wasn't there either and hadn't called in sick, although she'd been fine yesterday.

Not at home, not at work and her mobile was switched off. I didn't like that at all.

I made sure things were as I'd found them, then let myself out. I'd just have to wait for her. I went home and sent another message to the Boss, telling him what I'd done, what I'd found and what I was thinking.

What I was thinking wasn't exactly cheerful. The only friends she had in Bristol outside work were members of the Sisterhood, and if she'd gone to them for support, things might get difficult. I was now fairly sure that they'd slipped her something to set her off last night, and that some of it might have transferred when she kissed me. Hopefully there'd be some kind of residue in the blood now sitting in the fridge; I'd need to get that to the lab fairly fast if I wanted to know, and I'd asked for a courier to come and pick it up.

I spent the day waiting, not knowing what was going on. The courier came, collected and went. I tried ringing Annie several times, and always hit voicemail. I read files and formulated theories, and when night finally came I didn't sleep well.

I awoke the next morning in a less than happy frame of mind. There was still no word from the Boss, and Annie was still on voicemail. A quick check on her house found things exactly as I'd left them, and a neighbour told me she'd driven off on Thursday morning as usual and hadn't been seen since. I tried her work again, and was told that she'd phoned the previous afternoon to say she wouldn't be coming in any more. The guy on the other end of the phone sounded worried, too.

The penny finally dropped.

Back to the flat. Out with the files. Rifling through them to get employment histories for the whole inner circle. On with my best telesales voice, ringing each in turn with the 'You've won a prize!' routine.

Not one of them was in today. I tried their home numbers, with the same result.

I'd blown it. While I was sitting at home worrying about Annie and waiting for her call, all nine of them had made a run for it – and succeeded.

Knowing it was pointless, I sent a request to have their credit cards and car registrations tracked, and to have a watch placed at air- and sea ports. It was all I could do for the moment; that, and wait for the Boss's reaction.

To pass the time, I went through the files I had on the outer members of the Sisterhood. True to profile, they were nice, respectable women with ordinary jobs and apparently normal home lives.

Then the response came through from the Boss:

Cars registered to targets last seen on the A4361 entering Avebury. Local police now attempting to locate. Gather what intelligence you can and report back in person. Close Bristol phase of operation. Replacement vehicle can be collected from drop point nine, which is now your base of operations.

Zero. ///Ends

And with those words, Bill Freeman died.

I started slinging kit into a bag, stopping only to pull a plain black suit, white shirt and grey tie from the wardrobe. The gun went into a holster, and the little black wallet I kept handy for emergencies went into a pocket.

Drop point nine was an apparently semi-derelict unit on an industrial estate near Bath, where I was able to swap the nice innocent Golf for a nasty black Vauxhall with government-flagged plates. Leaving Bill's car behind me, I drove off and headed for Avebury.

One of the nice things about being official is the way you can ignore speed limits. The police will call your number plate in as they start to pursue, then back off suddenly when their control room tells them that the scary black saloon doing a hundred and thirty miles per hour isn't to be disturbed. With the tuned engine in my new car, I was outside Amesbury police station, a few miles south of Avebury, in not much more than half an hour.

The desk clerk had just finished dealing with an old

lady as I entered. Something about a lost purse, I think – not important. I removed my sunglasses and waited patiently to be called.

'Good morning, sir, how can I help?'

'I'd like to see the duty inspector, please.'

'May I ask what it's concerning?'

'Tell him Mister White is here from London. He's expecting me.'

The desk clerk did as he was told, then pointed me towards an interview room and said the inspector would be down in a moment. He was.

'Mister White, I'm Inspector Howard – what can I do for you?' Inspector Howard was a tallish bloke in his mid-thirties. He didn't look overjoyed to see a representative of what the plod call 'The Funnies' on his patch, and in his position I wouldn't have been either. It didn't help that I wasn't exactly overjoyed to be there myself.

'Eight cars, last seen on the northern edge of Avebury. Have you found them?' I was blunter than necessary, mainly to hide my irritation. Howard obviously didn't appreciate my attitude, but had the good sense not to mention it. Officially I wasn't there, he wasn't talking to me and the cars were a planned exercise sprung on the troops to see how well they were able to deal with a terrorist threat, or some similar bollocks.

'About half an hour ago, but the order only came through—'

'Take me there. Now.'

So we got into my car, and he did. Driving towards Avebury, I remembered how much I hate the place. Even though it's just a tiny little village, it's one of Britain's three great nutter magnets, along with Glastonbury and Stonehenge, and I'd managed to get myself damn near killed there twice. It's easy to let the hippies go on about how it's a blessed place full of light and love, but the entire area holds a history forgotten by many and not known at all to the greater part of the world. Thanks to all those standing stones, reality is thin around Avebury, and people have tried summoning things there on a regular basis for centuries. It's one of the reasons the Service was formed, actually: someone had to stop all those idiots from turning Britain into a council estate for every dodgy denizen of Hell and Faerie. Those first guardians were men of wisdom and learning, serving a higher purpose, but a few hundred years later, you get someone like me hurtling down the road in a suit and shades with a gun and a fake warrant card from Special Branch.

The small car park had been taped off with crime scene labels, and a group of men in white overalls were dusting the cars for fingerprints. Behind my sunglasses, I closed my eyes and let my mind expand for a moment. I could feel each living thing around me clearly through their pulses; then I shifted focus and started feeling for any psychic residue. There was none – they'd cleaned up behind themselves the same way I do. All I could hope was that the forensic examination of the cars would pay off, since it's an awful lot more difficult to hide DNA in a hurry – even when you know what you're doing. What I really wanted to know was which one Annie had travelled in, and what her current state of mind was. Knowing there was nothing I could do there, I had no choice but to head back to my new home.

Because the Service knows almost everything, and I have access to whatever information I need to do my job, I hate not knowing things. I especially hate not knowing where people are. But what had really tipped me over the edge on this one was guilt. I shouldn't have had sex with Annie, I should have realised that things were going wrong and there was no way I could excuse letting things go wrong for her like that. I was supposed to be her back-up, the one person who'd make sure she was safe. That trust had been broken when my dick took charge and I hadn't restrained her and got her out of there. I let her run off to who-knows-where and now she was missing, presumed held by the enemy.

But she was coming home. No matter what it cost, no matter who I had to go through, Annie was going to be all right.

I set about organising things. The windows of the unit were already light-sealed and while the place looked deserted, it was hardened to take a full assault and allow the occupants to hold on while the cavalry came down from Hereford to bail them out. That was where I planned to bring Annie once I'd recovered her, so I made sure that the medical supplies were in order, as well as the restraints. Unregistered phone lines made sure I had guaranteed secure links to the outside world for both data and voice traffic, so I could receive and assimilate whatever information came to light as fast as it could be passed to me. I had maps, photos, files and access to everything the British government knew.

What I didn't have was clue one what to do with it all. My mind was whirling with grief, guilt and worry – most unlike me under normal conditions. I lost the suit and stood naked in the middle of room, practising long-form t'ai chi until my mind cleared. It took a while, but I got there eventually. Time to stop worrying and start acting.

I looked again at the assembled data, trying to spot a pattern. As far as I could see, there wasn't one: all nine women had vanished off the face of the Earth pretty much simultaneously.

All nine of them . . .

All *nine*.

I went back to the desk, picked up the folders that dealt with the outer circle and started reading.

Chapter Seven

Jennifer Susan McNair was a pretty, successful advertising executive. Twenty-seven years old, she'd grown up in Exeter, graduated with a degree in marketing from University College London and moved to Bristol with her boyfriend straight afterwards. While the relationship didn't last long in the real world, Jen had done well for herself, accelerating up the corporate ladder at her agency, and she was now on the verge of promotion to deputy head of her department. Life was good. She'd just bought a large flat in one of the new developments, was seeing a nice young lawyer named Justin Marc Williams (who presumably hadn't told her about his conviction for public indecency after his entire rugby team mooned the Master of his Oxford college) and had been enquiring about getting a cat. A shiny new BMW convertible sat in her own space in the company car park and a platinum card covered her expenses. She was five feet five inches tall, with long dark brown hair and brown eyes. She wore a size 8–10 dress over a 32C–24–34 figure that was tanned from a recent holiday in Portugal, where she'd spent two weeks reading by the hotel pool and walking in the countryside. Her thirty-one-inch inside leg had helped immensely when she flirted with modelling as a student, and she was well liked at work and had an active social life. Her DNA held the gene for long-sightedness, meaning she'd need reading glasses before she was forty. She bought her food at Waitrose, clothes at a couple of chic places in London and her knickers from Marks & Spencer. She'd been a member of the Enlightened Sisterhood for three years, a hangover from an interest in Paganism while at university, but we didn't know how she felt about Annie being raised to the inner circle instead of her.

That life ended when I led a snatch team into her flat at three o'clock on a Sunday morning, drugged her while she slept, packed a bag of clothes and took her and her car away to a quiet little place in Berkshire.

Once she'd woken up, we left her to stew in her cell for a couple of hours while we watched on the cameras. There were no windows, although we left the lights on behind the translucent ceiling. She screamed herself hoarse, banged on the door and ended up crying, curled up on her bunk in the foetal position. Then we turned off the lights for half an hour, and she screamed again.

Jennifer's cell was six and a half feet square, with a bunk along the wall opposite the door and a bucket in the corner. Her clothes had been removed and there were no sheets. Everything was white, including the ceiling panels that the light came through. When the lights were on, the entire ceiling blazed just brightly enough to hurt the subject's eyes. In a couple of seemingly endless hours, that cell became Jennifer's private Hell.

Given the choice, I'd have let her spend a couple of days in there before we started asking her any questions, messing with her sense of time and making her as disoriented as possible, but the time wasn't there to play with. We'd have to work her over quickly, empty her of whatever she knew and then get rid of her. What happened to her afterwards would depend largely on her behaviour from this point on, but she didn't get to know that yet.

We let her go to sleep, then drugged her again and carried her to the interrogation room. She was strapped to a high-backed metal chair, and sensors were attached to her skin by the medical team. IV lines were inserted into each of her immobilised forearms, and a clamp held her head absolutely still, forcing her to look forward. Her peripheral vision was blocked off by blinkers, so she could see the desk and chair in front of her and nothing else.

Once everything was ready, a shot of adrenaline through the IV woke her up and set her pulse racing even before she was able to take in what was happening and be scared again. I was sitting behind the desk in a suit and tie, her file open in front of me so she could see what I was looking at. Panic raced across her eyes as she tried to move her head, look around, see anything but my quiet smile and her life laid out in between us. She whimpered.

'Hello, Jennifer.' I kept my voice calm, soft, almost comforting. It was the only voice she would hear from now on, and I wanted her to fixate on it quickly. 'You're wondering where you are, and what is happening to you. You want me to explain why you are here, and who I am.' I was stating the obvious, the things that were undoubtedly rushing through her panicking mind, but I was making it sound like a list of instructions; I wanted her to acclimatise to the idea that I was giving her orders and she was obeying them.

'Wh – What's—'

'You will not speak without permission, Jennifer. When I have finished you will have a chance to speak, but not until then.'

'But . . .'

I nodded to an assistant behind the chair who brought a cane down sharply between her exposed shoulder blades through the open chair back. She screamed.

'You will not speak without permission. Is that understood? Answer yes or no.'

'Yes.'

'Good. You will call me "Father". You are now in a place between life and death, between Heaven and Hell. What happens from now on depends entirely upon your actions here. If you please me, you will return to the world of the living and live the rest of your life in peace. If you displease me, then bad things will happen. The bad things have not yet begun, Jennifer, and I am sure you do not want them to. Do you want the bad things to happen, Jennifer? Answer yes or no.'

'No.'

'No, what?'

Her terror was palpable. Eyes fixed on me, she answered in a trembling voice. 'No, Father.'

'Good girl. Do you want to please me, then? Answer yes or no.'

'Yes . . . Father.'

'That is excellent, Jennifer. If you keep behaving like this, then you will please me. If you are obedient, and cooperative, then I will be pleased and all this will come to a swift end. That is what I want to happen, and that is what you want, too, isn't it, Jennifer? Answer yes or no.'

'Yes, Father.'

'So you want what I want, isn't that right? Answer yes or no.'

'Yes, Father.'

'Isn't that nice? I like a nice obedient girl. One who does as she's told. You *are* going to do as you're told, aren't you, Jennifer? Answer yes or no.'

'Yes, Father.'

I was amazed. I'd expected the process to take much longer than that, but obviously she had a weaker mind than the analysts thought. It was looking as if I'd already broken her; her eyes were lowered when I wasn't speaking, she answered quietly but clearly and seemed to be ready to tell me anything I wanted to know. There was a slightly dreamy expression on her face, as though a part of her mind was relaxing into this. It was time to press on.

'Jennifer, I am going to ask you some questions. You are going to answer them fully, without holding anything back. Some of them are questions I already know the answers to, and some of them are things I want to know. But you do not know which are which, and that is as it should be. If you lie to me, I will know, and you will be punished. If you tell me the truth, you will be rewarded. Do you understand me? Answer yes or no.'

'Yes, Father.'

'Then repeat to me what I just told you, using different words to show me you understand. Speak now.'

'I will answer all your questions as fully as I can. You will reward me if I tell you the truth and punish me if I don't.'

'And if you try to lie to me?'

'You'll know, Father.'

'That is excellent, Jennifer. You have pleased me.' She looked up, her spirits lifted a little by my praise. 'Because you have pleased me, you will be rewarded. Would you like to be rewarded, Jennifer? Answer yes or no.'

'Yes, Father.'

That was a signal to the assistant, who used a syringe to introduce a colourless liquid into Jennifer's bloodstream through an IV. Her eyes closed and her body shook slightly as the astonishingly addictive euphoric coursed through her. I closed the file, stood up and left the room, allowing her to enjoy ten minutes of orgasm in peace.

Next door in the observation room, I grabbed a cup of coffee (like any other Civil Service establishment, the tea was undrinkable) and watched Jennifer on the monitors. The techs were keeping an eye on her vital signs and preparing for her next session. They worked silently, although it was highly unlikely that Jennifer's conscious mind would be able to process any information at that moment. The shrink watching the session was fascinated by the speed of her compliance.

'Normally when we do this, it takes a couple of sessions to get someone into that kind of state. But she's fallen into it as though it's something she understands. Did you say she's been treated like this before?'

'Not as far as I know, but there seems to be some kind of kink theme running through the hardcore of the group, and it may well have transferred to the lesser members as well. You think she's enjoying this?'

'Judging from her reaction to the cane, it's a distinct

possibility. Keep the same attitude with her – firm and dominant. I'd say that's something she'd respond to without the treatment.'

'No problem. If she's willing to talk I see no reason not to just wipe her memory and let her go. Give her the usual: a bang on the head and a short stay in hospital. Then she can get back to her life and we can get on with the next thing.'

'Easy enough these days.' The shrink pointed to the monitor. 'You'd best be getting back in there, she's starting to come down.'

As Jennifer's vision cleared and her breathing came back to normal, she saw me sitting in the chair, smiling at her. It was a small smile, the sort of thing you'd give a child who's enjoying an ice cream – indulgent.

'Did you enjoy that, Jennifer? You may speak freely.'

'Yes, Father. Thank you.'

'That's good. That is what will happen when you please me. You want to please me even more now, don't you? Answer yes or no.'

'Yes, Father, I do. Anything you—' Then she screamed as the cane hit her back again.

'I told you to answer me yes or no. I did not give you permission to say anything else. Because you disobeyed me, you were punished. If you disobey me again the punishment will be more severe. Do you understand what I am telling you? Answer yes or no.'

'Yes, Father.'

'Very well. You do not want to displease me, Jennifer, and if rewarding you makes you disobedient, then I shall cease to do so. Obedience is paramount. You must obey my instructions without question, without thought, without any desire but to obey. Only then will you please me, and only then will you be rewarded. When I punish you it is to help you reach the reward, because only obedient girls are rewarded. Will you be an obedient girl from now on, Jennifer? Will you be obedient so that I can reward you again? Answer yes or no.'

'Yes, Father.'

'Good girl. Do you remember that I told you I have questions to ask you? Answer yes or no.'

'Yes, Father.'

'Do you remember the rules? If you do, repeat them now.'

'If I tell you the truth you will reward me, if I lie then I'll be punished. I mustn't try to lie because you'll know if I am.'

'That is excellent, Jennifer. I'm going to ask you those questions now, and if you obey the rules I shall reward you afterwards. Do you understand me? Answer yes or no.'

'Yes, Father.'

'Good girl. The questions begin now. You may answer freely until I tell you otherwise. What is your first name?'

'Jennifer, Father.'

'Good. With whom did you last have sex?' I threw that one in early to see how open she was really feeling.

'Annie Hargreaves, Father.' Annie? That was an answer I wasn't expecting.

'When and where was that?'

'On Tuesday night, at her house.'

'Was anyone else there?'

73

'No, Father.'

'Who initiated the sex?'

'She did, Father. She put a collar on me and made me do whatever she wanted. She used me all night.' Not that big a surprise after Thursday, but possibly an indicator of some kind of pattern. It certainly explained the mess her bedroom had been in.

'Had she been to a meeting beforehand?'

'No, Father. We met for drinks after work, then she took me back to her place for dinner. But there wasn't any food, so she said she wanted me for dinner instead.'

'What do you know about Sadie Hamilton?'

'She's wonderful. She taught me how to be a good little pet for the inner circle. Is Jennifer a good little pet for Father?' Another question answered: that was why she'd been so easy to break. She was conditioned to it already.

'You're an excellent little pet, Jennifer. Where did she teach you?'

'At Caroline's house in the country.' Caroline Blake was another member of the inner circle, but there was no record of her having any address other than a house in Bristol. 'There were lights, and music, and they made Jennifer feel good the way that Father does. They punished me for being bad, too, but I learned quickly because I wanted to please Mistress.' She looked quite proud of herself for that.

'Do you remember where Caroline's house is, Jennifer?'

'Yes, Father, it's ...' She looked blank for a moment, then worried. 'It's ... I can't remember, Father.'

'Jennifer, you just said you knew where it was. Now you're telling me you can't remember. Which is it?'

'I . . . can't remember, Father. I want to tell you, really I do!' She was getting agitated; the look of displeasure I was giving her obviously frightened her.

'If you won't tell me, Jennifer, I'll have to punish you – you know that, don't you?'

'But I don't know why I can't remember!' Panic was rising in her voice. 'It's got leaded windows and a red door and it smells of incense and I can't remember where it is! Please, Father, don't punish me!'

I stood up and walked out of her sight towards the door, signalling the techs to follow me. She was still screaming as I closed the soundproof door behind us.

'Please, Father, no! Daddyyyy!'

As the door closed, the lights in Jennifer's room went out and a computer-generated tone started to sound. Pitched at the upper range of human hearing and as loud as the front row of a rock concert, it would eventually drive the listener both deaf and insane. I had no wish to do that much damage to the poor girl, though. Hell, I hadn't wanted to do any of this. Thirty seconds would be enough to cause pain, nausea and complete disorientation, so after that I had the sound killed and the lights put back on, and returned to my desk.

'Can you hear me, Jennifer?'

She looked up at me with tears in her eyes. 'Yes, Father.'

'You were punished for not answering a question. Do you understand? Answer yes or no.'

'But . . . Yes, Father.'

'Now I want you to tell me the name of the house in the country where you learned to be a good little pet. You're going to tell me *because* you're a good little pet, my

75

special little pet.' I stood up and walked around the desk to stand in front of her. 'I know you want to be a good girl, Jennifer, I know you want to tell me. But wanting isn't enough.' I reached out and stroked her cheek. It was the first time she'd been aware of any human contact since she went to sleep in her own bed the previous evening, and she tried to nuzzle into the palm of my hand despite the restraints holding her head still. I looked into her eyes and smiled as she looked up at me with hope. 'There's a good girl. Now tell Father what he wants to know, and I shall give you an even better reward than last time – won't that be nice?' She smiled wanly, wanting to obey me, wanting nothing more than to make me happy, to earn her reward.

'Yes, Father. It's a house called … called …' Her face went blank again, then her eyes rolled back in their sockets and she started to convulse. The assistants had her chair folded back and the defibrillator ready before I'd registered what was happening. Despite everything they tried, Jennifer wasn't going to answer any more questions. She was dead.

As I came out of the interrogation room, somebody pointed me at a computer and told me there was a message for me. I entered my pass phrase and read what was on the screen, still slightly shocked by what had just happened.

Report to Chelsea safe house immediately. Zero. ///Ends

I got in the car and headed back towards London.

Chapter Eight

I walked the last five minutes to the safe house, having left my ride in the car park on Sydney Street. I circuited the block to make sure it was safe, entered the building and moved quickly up the stairs to the flat where this whole mess had started. It was empty, as expected, and I had nothing to do but sit around and wait for someone to show up. I grabbed a brew and started reading the newspaper I'd picked up at the newsagent's on the corner. All the usual rubbish was in there: governments posturing, politicians talking bollocks, pop stars hopelessly seeking the public's love; all the comforts of the real world in its desperation. It continues to amaze me that civilisation as we know it hasn't collapsed under the sheer weight of all the crap it produces; but then, holding that ridiculous edifice up is part of my job.

It took two hours of reading the paper and watching bad television before the Boss finally showed up. He didn't look happy at having been called out on a Sunday evening to see me, but then I don't think anything about his job made the Boss happy. Mine was certainly pissing me off at that moment.

'This meeting has just pulled me out of dinner with a bloody Cabinet minister,' he said, 'so if you want to leave this flat alive, you'd better have some bloody options for me.'

'Yes, sir.'

'Now, if I have this right, you've screwed the agent you were supposed to be backing up, lost all trace of the targets, irritated the Wiltshire Constabulary and even found time to interrogate someone to death!' His voice had been rising through this catalogue of joys, and he was now close to shouting. 'Perhaps you might have an explanation as to why you're not presently being loaded into a fake car crash to have *your* death explained?'

'Yes sir, the target estimates were wrong. There was a failure in the threat assessment and an insufficiently experienced agent was inserted into an environment she wasn't prepared for, or able to handle.' That did not seem to be going down well, judging by the look I was getting, but I didn't care. The Boss's mother might have done the threat assessment for all I cared at that point. It was off and somebody needed to say so.

'She was – *is* – an excellent agent,' spat the Boss. 'Her test scores were much higher than yours, for a start. Perhaps if you'd been able to keep your bloody trousers zipped up we wouldn't be in this mess at all! Or are you telling me that she wasn't last seen leaving your place naked except for an overcoat after the pair of you kept the neighbours awake for most of the night?'

'I still think something's wrong there, sir. I wouldn't normally have reacted like that ... Did she take Tantric training?' Some of our agents are trained in Tantra and sex magic, both as a background skill and for assisting them in getting close to targets. The rumour mill, in so far as we have one, says that they're probably among the most skilled lovers in the world, far surpassing anyone the KGB or any other agency could field.

'I believe so, yes. Why?'

'It would partly explain why I lost it so thoroughly.'

'Hmm. We'll see what she has to say later.'

'Later?'

'When you bring her back in. You are planning to get her out of there, yes?'

'Yes, sir. Of course I am.'

'Good. Do so. You'll be staying here overnight. Here's some reading.' He opened his briefcase and passed me a couple of folders. 'Toxicology report on your blood sample, forensics from Avebury and background data on Hamilton's American girl. Interesting reading. Oh, and just so you know, the pathologist who'll examine Miss McNair is on the secret list, so he'll be told to ignore the cane marks.'

'Thank you, sir.'

'There's a chap coming over to brief you in the morning about a couple of technical details you'll find in there –' he pointed at the files '– so be ready for him. After that, you're to find and eliminate the Enlightened Sisterhood and all their little friends. Bring Hamilton in for interrogation if you can, and I expect to see NF371 back here safely so we can sort her head out. You dropped a bollock there, and I want to know how and why. Is all that clear?'

'Sir.'

'Right, then, get on with it. The full moon's eighteen days away. I expect you to be done in fourteen tops. I don't want to have to tell the PM's people about this if I don't have to, so make sure I don't have to.'

'Right, sir.'

He put on his coat, picked up his briefcase and left without another word. Since I'd been awake for twenty-four hours, I decided to get my head down and read the files in the morning before the next briefing. Better to read with a clear head and actually remember what was going on than waste time having to read them twice.

I overslept. By the time I'd showered, shaved and made a cup of tea, there was a knock at the door. My meeting had arrived. He was a short, balding fellow in a grey suit, but his bearing practically screamed 'Uniform' to me. I let him in, gave him a cup of tea (milk and two sugars, oddly enough) and sat him at the table where he could spread his papers out.

'My name is—' I held my hand up, and he understood me: no names. 'Let's just say I'm an Army officer with a background in psychology and sociology, then. I've been asked to explain brainwashing to you, although I don't know why and have no wish or need to.' He looked at me expectantly, as though waiting for me to do something. 'You might wish to take notes.'

'I'll be fine.' I smiled and tapped the side of my head. He shrugged, presumably having seen this sort of thing before. I've got a pretty good memory, and took a course some time back to improve it. At times like this, I'm a sponge.

'Very well. While the roots of brainwashing technique can be traced to 1735 and an accidental discovery by a

Christian preacher during a "Crusade" in Northampton, Massachusetts, I think it's best if we begin with the work of Professor Ivan Petrovich Pavlov.'

'The dog guy.'

'Indeed. The work he did with animals led him to conduct research on human subjects, and he identified three distinct and progressive states of mind as part of the conditioning process. Firstly, we have the Equivalent Phase, where the brain reacts similarly to both strong and weak stimuli. Secondly, there is the Paradoxical Phase, where the brain starts to react more strongly to the weak stimuli than the strong. Finally there is the Ultra-Paradoxical Phase. This is the point where we see actual change; where conditioned behaviour and responses invert, negative to positive in therapy, or potentially vice versa if the programmer has other objectives in mind.

'As the subject progresses through each phase, the conversion takes hold more firmly. While there are many methods by which a subject can be brought through these phases, the most commonly used is to work on the emotions of a subject, bringing them to a state of profound emotional arousal such as anger, fear, tension or excitement.'

'What about pleasure?'

'I suppose so. The idea is to induce a state where judgement is impaired and the subject is more suggestible, and the more the state can be prolonged or intensified, the more it compounds.'

'Would drugs be an option to assist with that?'

'What's important is the state. Drugs, subliminals, charisma – how you do it isn't important, it's about keeping the subject there, stopping the brain from having a chance to rationally process the information, controlling their state of mind. I've seen records of the same results achieved using diet, physical discomfort, mantras, the revelation of shocking information, all sorts of things. To be honest, some mental hospitals use the same techniques in a thera-peutic manner.'

'And the longer you keep a person in that state, the more vulnerable they become.'

'Exactly – that's why big evangelists keep their audiences waiting. A combination of carefully selected music and the anticipation of what's going to happen can leave large groups of people in a very suggestible state, especially when the collection plate goes round.'

'I guess that explains the big houses they all live in, then. What happens next?'

'Once the subject reaches Catharsis, which is another name for the first phase, things get much easier and you can start the process of actually replacing their patterns of behaviour and thinking.'

'I suppose the mantras could come in handy there.'

'Indeed so. Getting them to reprogram themselves means you can have time for a cuppa.' He smiled. I didn't join in. 'Anyway, while the process works better in a long-term project, it can be done quite swiftly as long as there are regular reinforcement sessions. Would you like me to focus on either in particular?'

'The faster one, with top-ups. Would weekly meetings fit that profile?'

'Oh Heavens, yes. Weekly sounds ideal – normally you can only get away with monthly ones. They work pretty well, but the reinforcement on a weekly basis would give excellent results. With that kind of support, I'd say you could have the whole process in place within two or three days.'

'You're kidding me.'

'Oh no. I've seen motivational trainers who can do it in a day, as long as the subjects keep coming back. Otherwise the programming fades over time as the subject's old belief structure reasserts itself. Think of it as assaulting a position: you can overwhelm it at first, but if you don't secure it then the enemy can take it back just as easily. In this case that reinforcement is done by repeating the new idea to the subject in such a way as to make them absolutely convinced that their previous viewpoint was wrong, or else they'll start picking the new idea apart and finding things to disagree with. Once they start doing that you're stuffed, and the only recourse is to start the programming again.'

'Bloody hell.' That was something I had no idea about. I'd always thought that it took weeks of work to break somebody and mess their mind around. Now this quiet little man with his annoying voice was telling me that it could be done in a day. It was scary stuff, the kind of thing you hear about in conspiracy theories rather than the real world. Of course, I *work* in a conspiracy, so that just goes to show. My new friend the mad scientist continued.

'In the fast method, there are six basic techniques used to get results. Don't be surprised if you recognise some of them; after all, I went to Sandhurst and they use the same tricks there. The first is to ensure the process takes place somewhere remote, where communication with the outside world can be controlled. You're creating an environment where the subject cannot leave while the process is under way. Some people use agreements to encourage participants to complete the training, others just make it impossible for them to go anywhere else. Because it's a controlled environment, food, drink, tobacco and rest can be withheld, which will normally start altering the subject's internal chemistry. Hopefully it will also lead to a minor malfunction of the subject's nervous system and that helps the process along. Once they're locked in, by whichever means one uses, the actual work can begin.

'A schedule is introduced that works the subject for long hours without any chance for rest, causing them to become both emotionally and physically tired. You make sure there's no time to relax, and no time to think. Work them hard, work them long. Make sure that when the end of the day comes they can do nothing but collapse unconscious onto their bunk and then wake them up before they're properly rested. You also make sure that the environment is tense for the subject, and up their level of uncertainty. Put them on the spot at random, force them to tell their most intimate secrets to the rest of the group, anything that makes them drop their masks and become more psychologically vulnerable. A good bonding effect can be achieved if established members tell the subject secrets back. They don't even have to be true secrets, it just has to seem that way to the subject. Then you get a nice atmosphere where everybody trusts each other. But the trick about making them scared and uncertain is that it helps shift brainwaves into an alpha pattern, which is much more suggestible than normal consciousness. It's why talking somebody through a moment when they've frozen with fear works – you're able to skip around most of the mind's own defences and sneak the desired point of view in through the back door.

'The two last details are cultural. One is the use of language, incorporating jargon that the outside world doesn't use and making the subject feel that they're now part of a secret world that only the privileged few understand.'

'Would that include group activities?'

'Yes, certain group acts like eating particular meals together at meetings or singing songs that have been specially written would certainly be good. That helps keep the group cohesive, gives them an identity and increases the sense of belonging.'

'Ritualistic behaviour, that makes sense. What's the last?'

'Humour. Everything is deadly serious until the subject has "seen the light". After that, make sure there's plenty of laughter and such to help them see that things are so much better now. Suddenly there's happy music and dancing and all that; makes them truly appreciate the joy their new understanding gives them.'

'And you can do all that in a day.'

'With the right subject, yes. I'd prefer two, though, and the top-up meetings would be vital as well. Otherwise I'd want a month to give you results that would have a decent lifespan.'

'Where does hypnosis come into it?'

'It's not necessary. Although if you add hypnotic techniques to the mix, maybe recorded suggestions while they sleep, subliminal messages combined with properly structured background music, a mix of stimulants and antidepressants in the refreshments and a low-nutrient diet with the exercise the process becomes even easier. And that's before we get on to Stockholm Syndrome.'

'Hostages falling in love with their captors. I know that one. What about resisting this stuff? How difficult is it to fight off the influence?'

'Almost impossible. I read a report from a woman who was studying Vodou in Haiti. There was a part where she reported that the music in the temple started to cause her body to move without her conscious control and her mind entered an altered state of consciousness. Now, she knew exactly what was happening, and tried to get herself back under control, but anger or resistance just help the process along. The next thing anyone knew, she was dancing with the rest of the women and she awoke afterwards feeling "reborn". So even someone who's familiar with the process will be affected by it. The only defence is to get the hell away as fast as you can and not go back, because nobody sane can turn their emotions off so completely that these techniques won't work.'

'No defence at all.'

'Nope. Not a thing you can do. Once a subject's in that process, they're coming out different.'

'And you don't even have to strap them down, they just sit there and take it?'

'You can strap them down if you want to, but it's not necessary, no.'

His work done, the man left. I was amazed by what he'd told me. I knew it was possible to manipulate people with language and environment, but not that complete changes could be achieved so damned quickly. It was a frightening thought.

I decided to clear my mind by grabbing more tea and reading the files I'd been given the previous evening. Bad news all around: my toxicology screen was negative, and the cars told us nothing we didn't already know. Next was the background on Hamilton's ex. As I started reading, my eyes went wide and I started to understand exactly what the hell had been going on.

Chapter Nine

Once I'd opened the folder, the first thing that hit me was the cover letter. It was not, as I'd have expected, from the United States Air Force. This one came from the CIA. Among all the usual bullshit about inter-agency cooperation and the great holy War on Terror, and wanting to be all chummy and help out MI5 (who'd put the request in for us) were two pieces of pertinent and worrying information. Firstly, this file was so classified that the people photocopying it weren't allowed to look at what was on the pages, and secondly that this was a CIA personnel file for someone who had started out with the USAF.

Hamilton's ex was now a CIA agent. That was just what I needed to hear. At least she was an ex, which was a small mercy; if Hamilton had still had her for support it would have been a major fly in my ointment. But I'd asked for the file as possibly useful background reading, and I wasn't allowed to take it with me according to the stamp on the front, so on I went into the life of Captain Candace Alder.

The childhood stuff was dull, as was her early military career. She'd attended the University of California's LA Medical Center and qualified as a psychologist in 1980, then went on to serve with no real distinction in either direction in the US before she was transferred to RAF Greenham Common in 1985. When later questioned about her affair with Sadie Hamilton, who was an occasional member of the Peace Camp there, she admitted that they'd met in a pub near the base one night and things had snowballed pretty quickly. It was a passionate affair, full of stolen moments and narrow escapes from friends on both sides finding out that they were sleeping with the enemy in a very literal sense. The relationship had come to light when a love letter was discovered by one of Hamilton's friends and the gossip of the camp soon made its way to the security staff on base. Late one night, Alder found herself on a plane back to the States without even a chance to say goodbye to her friends in the medical block, let alone get word outside. While military men like to watch two women making out, it wasn't acceptable for either of them to hold a commission in the Air Force, especially if the other one was a commie.

On her return to the US, Alder had been charged with Conduct Unbecoming an Officer and given a chance to resign quietly before she was very publicly court-martialled and dishonourably discharged. At that point, the CIA had approached her to come and work with them, since psychology and behavioural science were all the rage: the FBI's recent successes with personality typing and suspect profiles had led their overseas counterparts to give it a go themselves as an adjunct to their existing psychological warfare techniques.

She'd laughed at MKULTRA and gone back to Pavlov's work on positive reinforcement, melding it with drug therapy and the Agency's standard brainwashing techniques. Her successes were notable, persuading militiamen to turn fifth columnist just for the chance to see her smile. She wasn't afraid to use her looks as part of the process, nor the promise of sex. In all, she seemed as ruthless as you'd want someone who warped people's minds and reprogrammed their personalities to be. There were rumours of her using the same techniques in her private life, and there was certainly evidence of a fair amount of patronage helping her career, especially from a couple of well-placed senators with a known fondness for spending leisure time naked and on their knees. Apparently, she'd been one of the minds behind blasting Noriega with music during the invasion of Panama in '89, and she'd been in the Balkans as a technical adviser during the nineties. Somewhere along the line, she'd received field agent grade combat training, scoring high in marksmanship and doing reasonably well in unarmed combat. The file was that of an exceptional woman, trained in any number of techniques to crush anyone who got in her way and turn them into her willing, even eager, accomplices.

I was starting to really not like the look of this at all.

She'd gone back to the US after the Balkans, working between a number of interrogation facilities – cracking people left and right. Co-workers she didn't like would transfer out or resign for personal reasons, and those she did like were exceptionally loyal to her. Looking at it from an armchair, I could see the pattern emerging; the Agency had effectively lost control of her, and she was indulging herself in any way she wanted. From inside, she must have looked unstoppable. Eventually she was transferred to the CIA holding and interrogation centre at Guantanamo

Bay Naval Base at the southern tip of Cuba. I couldn't help but think that a fair number of people breathed sighs of relief that day.

There was a photo of her from that time affixed to the sheet. Tall, slim and attractive, with black bobbed hair, a playful smile on her face and a hard look in her eyes. The climate obviously agreed with her, and her well-tailored black suit accentuated the light tan she'd have needed to work hard to avoid. She was a good-looking woman with few apparent morals in the conventional sense, let loose on a naval base that was cut off from the rest of the island. I could only imagine the fun she must have had. A number of naval personnel were transferred off the base at short notice after her arrival, a fact that came as no surprise to anyone familiar with her record but one that was carefully ignored by both the Navy and the CIA.

As the first prisoners from Afghanistan started to arrive, she was transferred to Joint Task Force 170 as part of their Behavioural Science Team. This marked a change for her, as it put her back under direct military command for the first time since she'd been pushed out of the Air Force, and she obviously didn't like it. They'd not listened to her suggestions, which then became demands. They'd sidelined her because she was a civilian, and because she was a woman. Her Air Force history came up, and her star fell further. Her requests for a transfer were ignored by Langley (who were probably glad to see her being reined in) and she was quickly prevented from having anything to do with the prisoners. Remarkably, her CO was able to resist where all others had fallen before and, despite a number of requests from his own staff, kept her firmly buttoned down. In late 2002, she resigned from the CIA, citing unprofessional attitudes from her colleagues and an opinion that the regime at Camp Delta (as it had become) was more interested in punishing prisoners than getting information from them, as evidenced by her own side-lining.

The CIA was glad to get rid of her. They gave her a new face, a new identity and the usual warnings about what happens to people who don't know how to keep their mouths shut. She was still flagged as being effectively under the protection of the US government, probably because she could open many cans of worms if she said the wrong thing. Any legal issues were to be referred to the nearest CIA field office, to be handled internally. Given her record, I guessed that would be about as much help as telling her she was a very naughty girl and not to do it again.

There was no record of the new identity in the file. The last picture of her had been taken just before she went into surgery. She looked much angrier there, the resentment at her treatment showing through without her making any effort to hide it. Her whole face seemed to be transmitting 'Fuck You!' through the camera. I wondered where she'd gone.

It was time to eat; I'd been reading for hours. Another ready meal washed down with tea killed my appetite, if not my desire for real food. I grabbed my laptop, logged on to the Service network and started looking at Hamilton's communication intercepts. Most of it was encrypted, and done well enough that she'd be dead of old age before we were able to read it. Open-source software and peer review had allowed the public to gain easy access to the sort of stuff we used to spend fortunes developing, and it hurt us badly at times like this. Most of the encrypted stuff was between members of the inner circle, but there were a few messages to and from the States. I ran a trace on the addresses and discovered their owners. None of them were even remotely likely candidates for Candace, but I put in a request for their files anyway. I checked the internet, trawling through the message boards Hamilton used but again couldn't see the pattern. It had to be there; the way Candace's file matched up with what was happening was too close to be a coincidence. There had to be some way for Hamilton to access her ex's work.

I needed to relax for a second, change tack and look at something else. When I get like this I find it's better to do something completely different and let my subconscious work undisturbed. I decided to go for a walk.

It was early evening as I strolled along the north bank of the Thames. Couples walked arm in arm, whispering sweet words to one another as joggers passed by plugged into their iPods. The sun was setting over London and a thin sliver of the moon was just visible, the last before New Moon. I had seventeen days before the full moon, and thirteen days before the Boss would have to tell the PM about the risk of an assassination attempt. Trouble was, I'd almost run out of places to look. The key had to be the house in the country Jennifer McNair had mentioned, but Britain has an awful lot of countryside. It would have to be relatively easy to get to from Bristol, I supposed, so that meant it would probably be in South Wales, the South West or the West Midlands. Possibly it would only be occupied part-time, so that might narrow things down as well. So far I'd resisted sending photos of the nine out to the police, since that would have drawn the kind of attention to Annie that policemen are liable to remember and not including Annie's details would have been worse. It was a bitch of a situation, but I'd sort it out. I always did; that's why I still had a job.

I ended up at a little restaurant off the King's Road, eating food I barely noticed and had forgotten five minutes after I'd cleared the plate. I hit a couple of bars and drank beer as my brain turned over all the possibilities. There had to be some means by which they were communicating. Maybe Caroline Blake was involved somehow – it was supposedly her house they were using for the conversions, after all. To take my mind off the thing for a moment I tried flirting with a couple of girls and came away with a phone number for my trouble. It was nice to know I still had it, even though I'd have been seriously bollocked for going any further.

Closing time saw me wandering back to the flat, checking for tails as a matter of routine. Nobody was trying to follow me, so the safe house couldn't have been compromised at least. If Annie had managed to hold that back, how much more didn't they know? Was it possible that they still thought Annie was just a normal secretary? I doubted it, but the lack of response from the Sisterhood might mean we were a little luckier than I'd thought. We'd see when I got her out. While stopping the Sisterhood's plan was my official first priority, I was starting to see saving Annie as my real one.

Back at the flat, I looked at the file again. Something

was missing. I needed to find out who Candace Alder had become, and where she was now. I could only think of one option; since the CIA wasn't going to tell me, I needed to ask someone who would. I just hoped he was still in London.

Chapter Ten

He was known by the people around him as Brutus. He was a huge black septic (sorry, African-American man), about six and a half feet tall, with muscle enough to make him bulky. He could have played American Football and been good at it, too. His mind, though, was his best point. Behind those dark eyes lay an incisive intellect that saw through people and problems alike. That had become his business: he was one of the finest information brokers in my world, and by far the most honest. It was said that he knew who really killed Kennedy, what was recovered from Roswell and exactly which burger bar Elvis was working in these days. It was also said that he'd been a US Navy SEAL and a hit man for the CIA, that he'd killed a hundred men and stormed the beaches of South-East Asia single-handed.

I knew that last part was bullshit. He had a body count of over seven hundred individuals, three governments and one demigod, and had worked mainly in North America, not South-East Asia. I knew this because he'd told me. I also knew that the first part was true, because he hadn't.

His shaved skull gleamed in the half-light of the club as he held court to the usual collection of misfits, weirdos and several astonishingly beautiful women. The three-piece suit he wore was fine tropical-weight wool from his tailor on Savile Row, only a shade blacker than his skin. The white shirt glowed between the lapels of his jacket in the ultraviolet light and his shoes shone like polished marble. A single gold earring caught the light as he turned his head to whisper in the ear of a blonde girl in tight black PVC hanging off his arm and she tilted her head back to laugh; unsurprisingly, the earring matched his tiepin perfectly. He knew exactly how good he looked because he'd spent a fair amount of his life arse-deep in mud and had decided never to look like shit again. In contrast, I was wearing my black 'Special Branch' suit, with a black T-shirt underneath. Among the denizens of this place, it didn't quite measure up in cut, tailoring, fabric or giving a shit about how fabulous I looked.

I worked my way across the dance floor, rock music shaking my eardrums as I passed between leather, lace and the bare flesh of the dark young things throwing themselves about or fondling each other as publicly as possible. A break allowed me to see a girl sliding her hand up another's skirt, then the vision was gone again, replaced by a muscled-up guy flaunting his nipple rings through a mesh top. Suddenly, the sea of dancers was behind me and the booth clearly ahead. I mounted the steps with a smile.

'Hamlet! My man!' Brutus's voice cut straight through the music.

'Hello, Brutus.'

'Hamlet here is the most miserable man I know,' he announced to the world. 'This guy could give the original angst lessons.' His minions tittered. Brutus had got used to dealing with people who didn't have names, and his literary inclinations had led him to assign his friends among that group names from Shakespeare. It suited me since I didn't know his real name either. 'Pull up a chair, old friend, and I'll introduce you.'

'I need a word, Brutus. Business.'

'Then you have an appointment for lunch tomorrow. Tonight, we party. Suzie, why don't y'all share your seat with Hamlet here while Seamus gets him a vodka?' A pretty, dark-haired girl in a black corset, spiky collar, ankle boots and not much else stood up to make space for me as a pale guy with long black hair went off to the bar. Once I'd settled down, she poured herself into my lap and threw an arm around my shoulders. Brutus smiled, apparently pleased with the arrangement.

'Y'know how Hamlet here and I met? I was fighting this Asian guy, real martial arts nut, had me up, down and sideways; hell, he had me beat before he got up that morning.' The group looked amazed that anyone could get past Brutus, let alone have him in a state like that. 'This man!' He pointed at me. 'This man steps out of a God-damned bush and shoots the fucker cold. One shot, one kill. Saved my sorry ass.' Suddenly, everyone was looking at me. That was pretty much how it happened, too, although Brutus did miss out the fact that his opponent was about seven hundred years old and he'd been warned to use a rifle rather than risk showing off and getting into the situation he had. I waved my hand: *no big deal.*

'Brutus exaggerates. I fired twice.' Laughter around the table. Suzie seemed to appreciate this information, squirming a little in my lap to get more comfortable. Since there was nowhere else to put it, I rested my hand on her knee; she didn't disapprove. My vodka arrived, and I settled into a little R & R.

The next morning came late for me. I awoke in a huge four-poster bed back at Brutus's place, with Suzie and a friend of hers whose name escaped me. We'd partied at the club until it closed, then adjourned to the huge house in Belsize Park (the posh bit of Camden) to carry on the festivities. There'd been drinking, and dancing, and somewhere along the line I'd ended up in a bedroom with two girls barely out of their teens, with all the enthusiasm and vigour of youth. We'd finally given up about an hour after dawn and collapsed into a sweaty heap of sleeping flesh. Brutus didn't need to keep his home a secret; he was too useful to everyone for it to be worth taking him out. I suppose I could have found out the name on the deeds, but it would probably have been fake and Brutus would consider it rude. Smart people generally tried not to be rude to Brutus. Not only that, the British government looked after him as a favour to the Americans because the big secret, the thing that made Brutus so well connected, the reason he knew so many interesting things and could find out so many more, had nothing to do with the SEALs, or the CIA; Brutus had belonged to neither.

Brutus was a retired Man in Black.

There was a quiet knock at the door, followed by the entry of Andrew, Brutus's assistant and a genuine ex-SEAL.

'Lunch is in twenty minutes. Would you like to borrow some clean clothes?'

'Yes, thank you.'

'Not a problem. You're what, a forty-two? Forty-four?'

'Forty-four regular. Thirty-four reg. trousers.'

'I'll get them up to you right away.' He withdrew, closing the door behind him. By the time I'd showered and shaved (there were things in the en-suite bathroom for such eventualities) the clothes were laid out on the bed: identical to what I'd worn last night, only about ten times the price judging by the labels. Leaving the girls still asleep, I headed for the dining room.

'Somebody had fun last night!' Brutus was all smiles as he clapped me on the shoulder and led me the last half of the way. 'Good thing you keep in shape, huh?'

'I guess so.'

'You should get out of that outfit, man, come work for me. I could use you.' Brutus's network of agents was legendary. It was a good place to retire to.

'Queen and country, mate. I'm not ready to go private just yet.'

'When every night could be like last night? You sure?' We both knew that every night would most definitely not be like that, but the idea was a fun one to play with.

'Get thee behind me, Brutus. There's work to be done.'

'Jesus, Hamlet, you've just been screwed all night by two nubile young things and all you want to do is talk shop. Damn, you're British!' We laughed at that until the food arrived. It was, as one would expect, top notch.

'So what is it you want to know?'

'Ex-CIA agent called Candace Alder.'

'Ooh, I know her. Well, her work, anyway. One scary lady. If I saw her, first thing I'd do is kill her. Don't let her even talk to you, man, that woman can have you barking like a dog in nothing flat.'

'The file didn't go that far.'

'It wouldn't, but I knew a guy who ended up working with her. Good man, with a family. By the time she was done with him, all he wanted to do was curl up in a little ball and sing to himself.'

'Shit. What had he done?'

'She caught him checking out her ass. Said she didn't like it and she'd make sure he never did it again.'

'That's better than good. That's magic.'

'You said it, brother. She's a head-shrinking, hypnotising, mind-fucking witchy-woman. Bad news.'

'She's involved in something, I'm sure of it.'

'Then tell me what you want to know.'

'When she left the Agency, they gave her a new identity. It wasn't in the file.'

'I'll bet. Langley won't want her cage rattled – they're terrified of the woman.'

'Well, I'm planning to rattle that cage, if I have to. I need to know who she is now.'

'This official?'

'Yep.'

'Fine, I'll bill your people direct. Good suit, by the way.'

'Thanks. It's one of yours.'

'Then you'd better keep it. You looked like shit in the other one. I'll put it on the bill. Do you need shoes to go with that?'

We finished lunch with tales of old battles and jokes about new conspiracy theories. I heard the latest gossip from around the world: who was up, who was down, who was about to be overthrown by his best friend and which politicians were being extra naughty this week. I threw him a couple of bits of trivial information back, since that was the way these things worked. Finally it was time for me to go and for Brutus to find the information I wanted.

'Look after yourself, Hamlet. You're too much fun to be dead.'

'And you're too beautiful, Brutus.' He took my out-stretched hand and pulled me into a bear-hug.

'I'll be in touch.'

I headed back to Chelsea, if for no other reason than I had to let the Boss know that another of Brutus's extra-ordinary bills was on the way. Catching my reflection in a shop window, I found that I had to agree with Brutus: the suit did look good.

It would be a few hours at least before Brutus had anything for me, so I started back through Candace Alder's file once again. I was still sure something was missing, something so obvious I was having trouble seeing the edges. I decided to take a nap, since the girls had taken it out of me somewhat and two or three hours of sleep weren't enough to recharge the batteries.

When I awoke, there was an email waiting for me from Brutus: a string of numbers, a user name and a password, and nothing else bar Brutus's initial and digital signature. The numbers were an IP address, the system the internet uses behind all the pretty 'www' nonsense. If you know where you're going, they work just as well as a web address; they also work very well if you don't want to make the server public knowledge, since all internet domain names are registered along with the owner's details and surprisingly easy to get hold of. I typed the numbers into my browser, then the credentials Brutus had supplied. Suddenly, Candace Alder's file appeared before me on the screen. I paged through the stuff I'd already read and found the point where my file ended. There was more in this version, a report that described her as a borderline sociopath with violent tendencies, a DNA profile (which I fed into the cross-matching database just in case) and details of her new life.

Candace Alder had become Susan James, and the CIA had set her up with a job at a small hospital in Illinois. She hadn't settled, though, and was soon up to her old tricks. There was mention of a doctor who suddenly liked to work naked, and a nurse who could only speak in rhyming couplets. Then she walked out of the place one evening and never came back. The CIA didn't know where she'd gone.

This was getting silly. I moved to the image files to get an idea of who we should be looking for. I opened the first file I came to, and the whole bloody thing fell into place and had me scrambling to write a message to the Boss. At least now we could understand why the Sisterhood had got the drop on us so badly. In the background, an alert popped up to tell me that the DNA was a match to a sample collected from one of the cars at Avebury. But that wasn't a surprise any more.

Staring out of the screen were the cool blue eyes of Caroline Blake, member of the inner circle of the Enlightened Sisterhood, and owner of that elusive little house in the country.

Chapter Eleven

There had to be a clue relating to the house somewhere, and it was now even more of a priority to find the place. I headed back to the industrial unit, where bits from the inner circle's houses had been delivered. For every day you get to stand in a circle and save the world, there seems to be about a week you spend going through some bastard's trash. Most of it was pretty unspectacular, standard commercial books on magic (some of which were actually pretty good for a change), social diaries, trade magazines and the usual ephemera you find around a magician's house. It was going to be a long night.

By about two in the morning I knew the ins and outs of everybody's credit card bills, washing machine guarantees and DVD player instruction manuals.

By three I knew everyone's favourite authors and what they watched on TV, having watched their video collections on nine televisions simultaneously as I searched the paperwork.

At just after four o'clock, the gods decided I'd done enough farting about and deserved a clue. I couldn't have agreed more and almost whooped when the grimy piece of paper fluttered out from a tatty copy of the *Malleus Maleficarum* and caught my eye: *Received with thanks,*

£2500. *23rd January 2005.* Followed by a squiggle of a signature.

It had come from Caroline's Bristol house, the one we knew about. It obviously wasn't one of her normal purchases, as she filed her receipts neatly in one of her desk drawers and I'd already been through them. This was somewhat shadier. Something about it looked familiar, though, as if I'd seen it before. Odd. I decided to hit the database and see if I could cross-reference it to previous cases. It would take a while, but I had nothing better to do and this would give me a bit of a sit-down away from the trash table.

'Receipts, handwritten, non-specific.' I typed the basics into the database and got a list of about three dozen names relating to cases I'd previously worked. Seeing no alternative, I set about looking at the scans of each, one by one, as the scanner beside me uploaded my new clue to the same database.

Second to last, I found the piece that this had reminded me of. A quick handwriting comparison confirmed what I wanted to know. I had a lead again, and would be heading north to see him in the morning. His name was Benjamin Eustace Daniels.

Benny was a dealer in artefacts. He'd started out in the antiques trade in the sixties, but then the black magic revival had come to his door and through a network of shady contacts he became the man to see if you wanted something and didn't necessarily want it noticed by the authorities.

Oddly enough, the authorities were one of his best

customers. Every so often, Piers would visit him with a briefcase full of used notes and a request for something I or one of my colleagues needed. Benny would hum and haw, then make a few calls and give a convenient delivery time that made you suspect that whatever it was had been in the back of his warehouse the whole time. Most of the major governments have repositories of major magical items, but Benny seemed to have sources everywhere and kept the trade moving.

I'd met him once before, when I'd had a word with him about a deal he was doing for twenty-five gallons of bottled water from the Fountain of Eternal Youth on behalf of a fading pop star from the sixties. The word in question was *no*. As I said at the time, we wouldn't have minded if it was *fake*.

Benny had a shop in Manchester, one of those dodgy backstreet antique shops that had been there for what looked like a thousand years, despite the fact that nobody ever seemed to pass by, let alone go in. There was yellow plastic covering the windows to stop the sunlight from fading things, peeling paintwork and a faded name across the top that had passed out of legibility sometime around the Norman Conquest. He lived in a flat above the shop that no mortal man was believed to have seen, but the odds were that it was just as grotty as everything else. The whole place was located in a notoriously unsafe part of the city, and designed to make the regular antiques crowd take one look and run in the other direction. Benny didn't want their trade directly; he preferred to put things quietly into auction when he needed extra cash rather than have people wandering round looking at his stock and asking where it came from. The only visitors Benny ever got were people seeking specific things, and an occasional hello from the Police Arts and Antiques Squad.

I walked through the door and into the half-light. Dust covered everything around me and hung in the air like a bad smell. It was said that occasionally people would buy stuff from the front shop, but the place was calculated to put passing shoppers and browsers off so effectively that even regular visitors who'd seen objects of some value in those piles tended to walk straight past them. Benny stepped out from behind a pile of original Victorian magazines and smiled at me hopefully. He was short, ugly and looked as if he was covered in as much dust as his supposed stock. His tatty tweed jacket had patches on the arms, and his glasses looked like they hadn't been cleaned in a year.

'Oh, Mister Chapman. Nice to see you again, what can I do you for?' His voice was soft and slightly effeminate, and trembled a little. He was justifiably frightened, as I had a look on my face that should have turned him to stone.

'Hello, Benny. Been speaking to any nice ladies lately?'

'Who, me, Mister Chapman? 'Fraid not. Business has been really slow lately, not much call for my sort of thing. All these chaos magicians using made-up stuff's been knocking a hole in me trade. People don't want the proper ritual kit any more.' Before he had a chance to complain any further, I thrust the receipt under his nose.

'Ring any bells, Benny?'

He sucked air between his teeth and fumbled for a cigarette. 'Can't say as it does, Mister Chapman. Makes you wish I kept books, dunnit? Then I could just look it up.' That, of course, was the reason why Benny didn't keep books. Magicians like their privacy, especially from other magicians snooping around what they're up to.

'Benny, Benny, Benny.' I sighed, wrapping an arm around his greasy, dusty shoulders. 'You might have noticed that I'm not in a very good mood. Had you noticed that?'

'Well, you didn't look very happy when you came in.'

'That's right, Benny, I didn't. And you not helping me out is just making things worse.' I reached to one side and pushed a crate of Georgian wine glasses onto the floor. Benny nearly jumped out of his skin. 'Now, Benny, look at that. I can get clumsy when I'm irritated, and you've got some lovely stuff in here. Wouldn't it make things easier for everyone if you had a nice think and told me about the lady who came shopping?'

'You know I don't talk about my customers, Mister Chapman. It's the rules.'

I shook my head sadly as I kicked a wrought-iron hat stand into a very old grandfather clock that had been ticking away merrily to itself.

'Are you sure, Benny?' I turned him to face me, resting my hands on his shoulders. 'Are you really sure that you want to make me any more upset than I already am?'

'Oh, come on, Mister Chapman, there's no need for all this!'

I stopped and thought for a moment. 'You know what, Benny? You're right, there isn't.' I punched him in the face and heard the crunch of cartilage as his nose broke. 'There's no reason at all for me to piss about and let you weasel around when I could just cheer myself up by beating it out of you.' Benny's reply was incoherent, but seemed to revolve around the word 'no' quite a lot. 'What's that, Benny?' I grabbed a handful of hair and lifted him to his feet. '"No", was that? Was that "no" as in "please don't hurt me I'll tell you everything you want", or "no" as in "I'm a stupid little shit and I want you to hurt me very badly"? It's difficult to tell.'

'Please, Mister Chapman, I can't tell you. It's my reputa—'

I kicked the back of his knee and sent him sprawling into the broken glass.

'Do you know, Benny, that you are one of the most disgusting things I've seen in this dimension? I mean, look at this place.' I shoved another box of priceless antiques onto the floor next to Benny's head with a crash. 'It's a fucking tip. A death-trap, even. You never tidy up, the place looks like it ought to be burned down by the Public Health Department and you're just as grotty as the rest of it.' I stamped on his ankle and he screamed. 'Now then, why don't you start by telling me exactly what you sold Caroline Blake? Answer the first question, and it gets easier from there.'

'Please, Mister Chapman, don't!' I kicked him in the balls. 'Mirror! It was a mirror!'

'What sort of mirror?'

'Big old thing, silver-backed, antique.'

'Good boy, Benny. That wasn't so hard, was it? Did you deliver it?'

'I can't, I really can't—' Another kick in the balls. The second one always hurts ten times as badly, and with the amount of force I put into it I'd be willing to swear that Benny could now hit a top C.

'Wrong answer, Benny! Did you deliver it?'

'Yes! Yes!'

'Where?'

'Don't make me say! She'll kill me if she finds out!'

'What makes you think I fucking won't?' I picked up a convenient poker and hit him with it, hearing at least one rib break. 'Do you doubt my resolve, Benny?' I hit the other side of his chest and another rib went. 'Do you somehow think I'm going to stop now just because you ask me nicely?' I grabbed his wrist and started dragging him to a mangle in the corner of the room. 'You play violin, don't you, Benny? You're pretty good from what I hear.'

'Y-yeah. What's that got to—' He saw the mangle. 'Oh fuck, no! Please, Mister Chapman!'

I pressed his fingertips to the rollers.

'Just name the place, Benny, and I stop.' I got a good grip on the handle and gave it an experimental turn. The rollers moved much more easily than I'd expected, with decent traction on poor Benny's fingers. 'Your choice.' He looked up at me, his face pleading for mercy even as he gibbered incoherently. I kept my face set as if it was made of stone, looking down at him as if the Last Judgement was under way. 'Last chance, Benny.'

'Pickerell House! Temple Cloud! In Somerset!' I let his wrist go.

'Thank you. I'm going to assume that you're telling me the truth, Benny, because I think you can probably guess what's going to happen if you're not. While you may be a shit, I don't think you're quite that stupid. You're not that stupid, are you, Benny?' I didn't get an answer. Benny was sobbing and gasping for breath, curled into a ball on the floor. His breathing didn't sound too good. I went behind the counter, emptied the cash box to give the police a nice easy motive and went outside in search of a map.

It was a relief to be back in the real world after Benny's hole, although the stink always hung around my nostrils after I'd been in there. First thing to do was find a phone box and call him an ambulance; I didn't want him dying if he didn't have to. Hell, I hadn't wanted to hit him, either: he was just a poor, stupid little man who'd got himself caught up in something way over his head, and not for the first time. I wished he'd had the good sense to do as I'd asked at the beginning, but the truth was that he couldn't. He was as trapped into that beating as I was into delivering it. Hopefully there'd be no hard feelings, but I wouldn't blame him if there were.

My next port of call was a decent bookshop for a map of Somerset. Temple Cloud turned out to be a small village near Midsomer Norton, just a little south of the Stanton Drew stone circle. I had to give our friends points for style, picking a village with a name like that. It was almost certain that there would be some connection to the Knights Templar, considering where it was, but I doubted that anything like that would be relevant in this case. There seemed to be a couple of places beyond the outskirts which looked as though they'd be my best candidates for Pickerell House, but that would be easy enough to check locally when I got there. First job would be to reconnoitre the area, see who was there and decide how to proceed. There'd be back-up if I needed it, but I'd rather do the job alone if I had the chance to. Getting Annie out would be the challenge, though.

Chapter Twelve

Having dropped the contents of Benny's till into a handy charity box, I drove back to the industrial unit as if the fires of Hell were heating my arse. It was about teatime when I got there, and I packed kit swiftly. Check, recheck, into the bag. Night-vision goggles, surveillance gear, ghillie-suit base, matt-black combat gear, webbing and weapons. All the tools of the trade. I screwed the suppressor onto my pistol carefully, then repeated the procedure with my sub-machine gun. Suppressors are a pain in the arse for anything beyond close range, but I have enough faith in my stealth skills and ability to get close enough to risk using them. I never was a sniper, and their black arts are as much of a mystery to me as mine are to them. Plastic bags for bodily waste, just in case I had to lie up for a while, and a couple of days' worth of food and water. Binoculars with anti-reflective lens shields and built-in camera and rangefinder. Secure radio with good crypto and burst-transmission capability, to let the Boss know what was going on and to call the boys in from Hereford if it looked too tasty for me to deal with on my own. All this sat, with spare ammunition, in my webbing and a small daysack. The final touch was to check the edge on my beloved Sykes-Fairbairn commando knife, to my mind the finest hand-to-hand weapon in human history. With that slipped gently into its sheath, my kit was rigged and ready to go. I sent a message back to let the Boss know where I was going and why, threw the lot in the car and headed south as the sun was setting.

I left my car in a lay-by near South Hinton, a couple of miles from the target. I'd got the exact location from the car's satellite navigation on my way back down from Manchester, and we'd even managed to fly a spotter plane over the house from a local airfield once I'd confirmed the location, so I had a couple of aerial photos for good measure. One large house and what looked like an old stable block to the right as you faced the front door. Gravel out front and down the drive, which had a sharpish ninety-degree curve to the road that would be a nice shield against prying eyes. It was surrounded by open grass, with a stream about thirty feet away on the south side but, more usefully, a small wood to the north. That struck me as an ideal place to lie up and get a look at the place.

Once I'd got my shit together, I struck out for Pickerell House, moving a little slower than usual to minimise any disturbance to the locals. I spent an hour in the woods, too, picking foliage and attaching it to my camouflage gear. While a standard camo pattern can break up your silhouette a little, there's nothing like actual local terrain to keep you from attracting attention, especially when it's attached to you. Then it was quietly through the woods to a reasonable vantage point. By the time I was in position it was past midnight, so I settled down for a bit to take in the scenery and wait for the right moment to scout around a little more.

The last light went out at about two, so I waited another hour before I broke cover to get a decent look at the buildings. My main problem was caused by the stable building – it had no windows on the side facing me and blocked my view of the front of the house. With the gravel out front as well the whole thing was risky. I was going to have to rethink things a little on the fly. A large bush next to the drive looked like an option, so I went to check it out. Good-sized, it had the advantage of a clear view of the front of the house, but to counter that it was plastered in thorns which would make getting out in a hurry difficult. It was still the only viable choice, and put me about fifty yards from the front door of the place. As long as I was careful, and didn't need to move fast, I'd be fine.

By the time dawn started to show in the east, I was all sorted out. I was lying in a shallow trench, covered by a plastic sheet which had earth and vegetation stuck to it so it blended in with the ground. A Wolf's Ear directional mike pointed at the house, and apart from that and my shielded bino lenses there wasn't a single trace of my passing. I'd done my final escape and evasion test with the Gurkhas hunting me, and passed alone out of fifteen people. Mud and dirt didn't bother me because they were my friends, just like the insects crawling on my back and the bird sitting on top of the bush announcing the sun's return at the top of his voice.

Nothing happened for a couple of hours, during which time I carefully got some food down my neck and started thinking about ways of penetrating the house. It wouldn't be easy: I'd need to catch them all together, ideally, and take them fast with the SMG. It would have been easier with stun grenades, but I didn't have any. I don't particularly like them, any more than I like tear gas or any of the other assault gear the Army boys use. I appreciate a good explosion as much as the next bloke, but I've always prided myself on using stealth over force. The best weapon anyone can carry is a good brain, and I prefer to use that rather than guns, grenades and all that jazz.

The house started coming alive at about seven. Lights went on in what I felt I could safely assume were bedrooms and I scribbled names next to windows on my sketch map as curtains were drawn. Then the headphones started feeding me sounds of activity from inside the house. I got the impression that there were seven people in there, but while I could hear sounds of speech, the walls were too thick to make out any words. All seemed well, though; the voices sounded happy and unconcerned. It was shaping up to be a sunny morning, and from this position all I'd be able to do was sit, watch and wait.

Activity through the day was light. Occasionally, one or another member of the coven would stroll out of the house for a walk, and at lunchtime someone took the battered Volvo parked by the house away and came back with shopping. Judging from the time it took, I guessed they were using a local village shop. That made good sense, as we'd have tagged them on CCTV the moment they came within range of a camera in a larger town. I'd never doubted how smart these people were, and this was just another example of that.

By this point I'd come to the conclusion that I only had two options for dealing with the situation: sneak in at night and kill them in their beds, or call in the strike team and hit the place like an embassy. Neither particularly appealed: calling in the heavy mob for back-up could lead to complications for the Service both politically and operationally, since anything that major would probably attract unwelcome attention from MI5 or the media – which is bad news for an outfit that doesn't officially exist, and despite what the Boss thought I didn't exactly relish creeping through the house with a knife like a serial killer. But as the saying goes, if you can't take a joke, you shouldn't have joined. I started considering options for penetrating the house quietly.

As the sun came down, the front door opened and the women started to file out in plain black robes and head towards the stable. Hamilton was at the front, wearing a silver medallion, followed by Caroline in the number two position. Annie was second from the back, not looking at all happy about the situation. That was good news – she was still alive and her cover was intact. I wondered why she hadn't tried making a break for it, but came to the conclusion that she was keeping them quiet and happy until I was able to catch up with them. Good girl, I thought, looks like she really is developing the spine for this game after all.

They were in there for a while, and I could just about catch the sounds of call-and-response chanting, bells and all the standard ephemera of a fairly normal-format cere-mony. Candlelight flickered in the stable windows and I could dimly make out the shape of somebody's back through the window. What was annoying was that this was the best angle I could get on the terrain without being over a mile away, and I preferred to be close. After a while the sounds inside the stables changed from those of basic ritual to what was definitely sex, and the wind started to pick up. Clouds rolled in from the horizon, darkening with rain as they approached. Within a couple of minutes it was raining, and as I heard the first orgasm inside lightning streaked across the sky. The plastic and the bush kept me pretty dry, fortunately, and the lightning hadn't come close to the house yet. I finally realised what their role in the assassination was – to stop the PM being evacuated by air. There was no way anyone could get a helicopter through that kind of weather, and that would leave the target stuck to the ground, where he could be got at. Personally, I thought it was a bit showy; I'd have waited for him to evacuate and then taken the chopper out with a couple of missiles, but maybe showy was what they wanted. It would be good cover for ground units as well, so that might also have been a factor. If the game went all the way to the end, then hopefully I'd be able to make good use of it if I had to go hunting on the night.

After an hour or so the moaning in the stables died down and I could hear them doing the final banishing. Shortly after that they came out, naked and obviously sweaty, to be washed off by the rain that was still falling pretty heavily as they made their way back into the house. A couple of them seemed to have a little trouble walking, although whether that was caused by cold, drugs or still-wobbly knees I couldn't tell. It had obviously taken a lot out of them, though, since bedrooms lights started going on shortly afterwards and the house was quiet by eleven. I waited until about two o'clock before I made my move, long enough to make sure they were all thoroughly asleep.

I decided to wear the camouflage up to the entry point, to help keep me dry if nothing else, and to leave the SMG behind. I was only carrying the pistol as back-up in case I discovered more than one of them in the same bed. I slowly slid out from the bush, rain covering any noise, and made my way down to the riverbank, hiding in the darkness.

I selected a window at the side of the house, covered by the Volvo, and looked for alarms. There was a sensor strip along one side, designed to detect the window opening and attached to a fairly solid-looking bolt. Less than ideal. I examined the rest of the window and decided it was worth risking removing the pane from the lower half. A small container of acid helped the putty come clear of the frame and I carefully placed the glass sheet out of the way. Shedding the camo, I moved inside.

Stop, evaluate, think. I had no idea of the internal layout of the house, so would be winging it from thereon in. I was in a chintzy living room, with two sofas, a low table and a lot of bookshelves. Two doors, one directly opposite me that presumably led into the entrance hall, and another that led towards the back of the house, maybe to the kitchen. Try the kitchen first, as you don't want anyone coming up behind you if it can be avoided. That was a good way to end up with a paintball in the back during training, and a gravestone on your head in the real world.

The kitchen was empty, as were the hall and the other main downstairs room. Time to move upstairs. Placing my feet carefully on the edges of each step to avoid creaks as I climbed. Movements slow to make sure my weight transferred smoothly from step to step. Into a corridor with two doors towards the front and three to the back, stairs in the middle of the floor meaning I'd have to choose a direction and recross the stairwell to continue, another flight of stairs leading up to an attic conversion. Pick a target: first on my left, to the front of the house.

One woman in the bed, snoring quietly. I slid my knife quietly from the sheath, keeping it carefully balanced in my hand. Slow, gentle steps took me to the bedside. I looked over to see her face. Amanda Patrick, a forty-two-year-old pharmacist. I checked my position and drew the blade across her throat, angling it so that the arterial spray missed me. Her eyes flickered open, then a look of terror crossed them as she realised she was dying. No sound bar the air escaping from her severed windpipe. It didn't last long; her body shuddered as she left, and then stopped moving entirely.

Out of the room, across the hallway to the rear-facing room. Again it was a single occupant. The same procedure: slow, careful approach, identify the lump under the quilt as Mary Shaw, a shop manager originally from Australia. Change position slightly and push the blade into the top of her neck, severing the spinal cord. Unable to move, even to breathe or make her own heart beat, she would be dead inside a minute as her brain ran out of oxygen. By the time that happened I had crossed the stairwell and discovered the bathroom.

I had two doors left on this floor. Deciding to continue working in a circle, I drifted quietly into the last rear-facing room on the first floor. A careful approach to the bedside to look at the next woman's face. Annie.

This put me in a difficult position. I hadn't decided when to wake her up; whether to let her sleep as I finished the group or get her out as I continued. Before I realised what I was doing, I'd put my hand over her mouth and she was waking up. Her eyes widened in terror and I remembered the night vision goggles and balaclava I was wearing. I pulled them off to show her my face, and terror turned to surprise.

'Bill!' she whispered. 'What the hell are you doing here?' Her eyes flickered to my knife.

'Getting you out. We're rolling this up.'

'But . . . How many have you done so far?' Something wasn't right about the tone of her voice. I wasn't sure what, but something was wrong.

'None. I'm to extract you before the strike team gets here. We've got about half an hour.'

'Right. So you're alone?'

'Not for long. The Boss wants us clear before the boys arrive. I'm to get you out, disable the alarms and then we go. OK?'

'Right. Hand me my coat, will you?'

'Sure. There's a large bush by the drive, hawthorn, I think. Meet me there in about five min—' As I turned back with Annie's coat, something hit me hard in the middle of the face, and I just about felt the ground come up to hit me as the world went black.

Chapter Thirteen

Pain brought the room back into focus. My face hurt as though somebody had decided to remodel it with a curling stone, my ears were still ringing and my eyes could only open a crack to let me see what was going on. I was lying on the floor of Annie's room, blood sticking my face to the carpet. A quick check confirmed the expected information: my nose appeared to be spread across my face. Again. Just what I needed, since it meant that I'd now have so much scar tissue up there that someone would have to drill me out a new set of sinuses. There appeared to be nobody else in the room, and the house was quiet. Peeling my face off the floor, and ignoring the pain for a moment, I took a look around. Annie had left in a hurry, and I could see that the occupants of the room opposite had done likewise as both doors were now open. My head swam a little as I stood up and started piecing together what had happened. No matter how I looked at it, the answer was obvious: Annie had put me down. According to my watch, I'd been out for around an hour. That wasn't good, and I'd need to be checked out when I got back to civilisation. Knocking someone out is neither as easy nor as safe as it looks in the movies. To do it successfully, you've got to hit them pretty damned hard, and there's a serious risk of permanent brain damage.

Once I'd looked in the mirror, I knew what she'd tried – driving my nose up into my brain for a kill. Luckily for me, that's a really difficult thing to do, and it was a stupid move for her to have made. In her position I'd have been inclined to go for a punch to the throat; it's a lot easier and far more likely to cause lethal damage. As it was, I'd have been more likely to drown in my own blood if I hadn't fallen in the recovery position. Obviously not time for me to go just yet, then. But Annie was going to have a fairly large amount of explaining to do next time I caught up with her.

The bleeding seemed to have stopped, so I started searching her room. Nothing of any interest there, just a few clothes and a book of the *Why All Men Are Bad and All Women Are Good* ilk. It was apparent that she'd packed a small bag and made a run for it, and this was the pattern I found in the room across the hall, although it looked as though two people had been asleep in there. I'd been banjaxed. Fooled. Fucked over. Annie had gone native and joined the other side; there seemed to be no doubt about that now. Something had happened after she joined the inner circle and I wanted to know what it was, especially since it had cut through the Service's own conditioning – which I'd been relying on to keep Annie's personality intact under her cover identity. More importantly, she now represented a danger to me, and to the Service. She knew enough to cause an awful lot of trouble, and if word got out into the public domain about who we were and what we did, the Service would be shut down in a heartbeat. I had no illusions about what that meant: the field staff would be wound up and removed from circulation double-quick. I might be lucky enough to get Brutus to take me on if that happened, but whether or not he could protect me from a hit team if one came looking for me was another matter entirely. Maybe it was time to get out early after all.

The most important thing to do was clear the house before I searched any further. Quickly and quietly, I flitted from room to room, making sure that nobody was waiting behind to give me a nasty surprise. As I'd expected, it was empty: they'd seen the chance and taken off before my mythical back-up arrived. I suppose I was lucky that Annie had never worked with me before and didn't know that I prefer to do this kind of thing on my own.

With the house safe, I allowed myself the luxury of some choice profanity and a scream as I pulled my nose into a reasonable facsimile of straight. Then I made my way back up the staircase to start a decent search of the place from the top down before I called in the forensic boys.

I heard a movement in the kitchen.

That was bad. I froze and opened my ears to the world. Soft, slow footsteps at the back of the house, and now a set in the front room. I drew my pistol in a single fluid motion and moved as quietly as I could to the first landing. My best hope was to take them from there, using the banisters and corridor for cover. I drew a bead on the base of the staircase, took a deep breath to relax and waited for a target to present itself.

A minute passed that felt like half an hour. Whoever was down there was moving patiently, obviously clearing the floor the same way I had. I could hear soft sounds of movement below, and then a creak above me. I'd been boxed in. I'd checked the top floor, but somehow I must have missed a hiding spot. My best option now was to move to Annie's room and defend from there. If I called the cavalry, I'd need to hold out for anything up to an hour, and I didn't have a huge amount of ammunition. That said, even if all seven of them came at me together I'd have enough to take them. Probably. Decisions, decisions . . .

My first decision was to stop sitting in the open like a lemon. I slowly rose to my feet and started for the end of the corridor. As I did, I heard something land behind me. A stun grenade. Leaping for the nearest door, I was halfway through as the thing went off, filling the area with blinding light and a bang that left me with only a high-pitched whining to listen to. I staggered round and started to bring my gun up towards the black figures in gas masks who were pointing sub-machine guns at me. They were waving their hands at me, and presumably shouting something I couldn't hear. Then the penny dropped and I let my gun fall to the floor. I had to hope that this was what I thought it was. 'Cutter!' I shouted, loud enough that I could almost hear it. 'Cutter!' I was pushed to my knees and someone cable-tied my wrists together. It hurt like hell when added to everything else, but at least I wasn't dead so the recognition code might have worked. I decided to go with the only sensible option I had under the circumstances and passed out.

I woke up somewhere quiet. I was in bed, on clean sheets, and seemed to be in no imminent danger of death. Good news. Everything hurt like a bastard, but that didn't exactly come as a shock and by the look of things (and the smell of disinfectant) I was probably somewhere that had painkillers. I have a weird relationship with painkillers: if you told a doctor what my average consumption was over the course of a year he'd probably recommend rehab, but they're always prescribed and I manage to go months without them. It's just that I get the crap kicked out of me on a regular basis doing this job, and when those times come around the opiate family are as welcome as a rich uncle who's about to kick the bucket. I lay back, closed my eyes and waited for someone with prescription authority to drop by. Somehow I must have drifted off to sleep, but then it had been a trying couple of days.

The sound of movement in the room brought me back. One person, presumably female since blokes tend not to wear high heels. Presumably not a medic for the same reason. I opened my eyes a little to see what I could see.

Ankles.

Nice ankles, in a pair of plain black middle-range shoes. Not cheap, but not exactly Jimmy Choo, either. Well-shaped calves, too: someone who took a reasonable amount of exercise. The black hosiery was a nice touch. My view ran out just below the knee, but I liked what I'd seen so far. Time to open my eyes a little further.

Nice knees, and a grey tailored skirt that gave a damned good account of the thighs underneath. Trim waist, jacket to match the skirt. I kept liking what I was seeing: obviously fit, toned and healthy. Well-proportioned bust kept professionally under wraps, and the back of her head showed blonde hair of uncertain length done up in a bun.

She looked as if she'd just stepped out of a boardroom in the City, which probably meant she was a lawyer. I don't like lawyers, no matter how sexy they are, so I put that thought to one side for another second or two and enjoyed the view.

Maybe I was dead, and this was Heaven's welcoming committee. Unlikely, since the ideas I was getting would have sent me straight to Hell. Besides, I'm pretty sure you don't get lawyers in Heaven. I decided to admit to consciousness, mustered up what charm I could under the circumstances and smiled as I greeted her.

'Hello there.'

She turned round to regard me. Full red lips parted in a slight smile and her ice-blue eyes looked straight into mine.

'Good afternoon, Major White.'

Fuck.

Penelope Marsh, late of the Army Intelligence Corps and now a member of Her Majesty's Security Service (MI5 to us mere mortals), was reading my medical notes.

'Or should that be "Captain Harris"?' she continued. 'That's what it says here, anyway. I don't suppose you happen to have any identification handy, do you?'

'I don't have anywhere to put it, Miss Marsh.' I spread my hands and smiled. 'Seem to have mislaid my uniform.'

'Hmm.' She didn't look happy. While I'm sure she did occasionally *have* good moods, they didn't tend to happen around me. If you knew our history, this wouldn't come as a shock. She was under the impression that I was Army, as you'll have probably guessed from all the rank bullshit, and a member of the 14th Intelligence Detachment, a quiet little corner of the Intelligence Corps that deals with the nasty things best seen to quietly. She'd got out when she was a lieutenant, but with flawless Civil Service logic it had been decided that a desk jockey would be the perfect liaison officer to deal with people who spent weeks at a time up to their arses in shit. As a result of this, she looked down her nose at me and I pretended to look down my nose at her – the poor girl didn't even have the clearance to know my long-term cover name, let alone what I really got up to. She was an irrelevance, albeit a very attractive one. If it were possible I'd have sent her away with a flea in her ear, but because I'm officially an anti-terrorist operative (for the purposes of the Army, at least) there has to be some occasional pretence at cooperation. Grudging cooperation for preference.

'Care to explain what you were doing in Temple Cloud, "Captain"?'

'Not really, no. Why are you here?'

'Five are supposed to be briefed on anti-terrorist operations on the UK mainland before they happen. We're *not* supposed to find out about them when the SAS are scrambled for a rescue mission!' Her cut-glass tone was sexy as hell. It was more like being told off by a strict schoolteacher than the righteous bollocking she meant it to be. All I could think of was bending her over my knee, and the resulting smirk couldn't have been as well hidden as I'd intended because her eyes darkened and her voice got louder. 'If you don't start telling me exactly what the fuck you were up to in there, I'm going to make sure you're on the end of so much shit you'll be ten years past retirement before you see daylight again!'

I love it when she talks dirty.

The bitch of it was that I'd read her record. She'd done pretty well for herself, and bagged a fair share of bad guys. Being stuck in a desk role wasn't what she wanted, and I could understand her frustration at being on the edge of all the fun stuff without anyone wanting to tell her what was happening. But sympathy doesn't count for much in the real world, and all I could do was add to her frustration.

'I'm sorry, Miss Marsh, but I'm not able to discuss operational matters with you unless I get clearance from my commanding officer. Why don't you go and look for yourself?'

'Because your mates won't bloody well let me!'

'Shouldn't you take that as a hint? Perhaps if you put a request through the proper channels—'

'Oh for fuck's sake, White – or whatever your fucking name is – why can't you just play ball this one time? If we don't know what's happening, how are we supposed to help?'

'What makes you think—'

'Fine, stay out of it, then. Either way you know this isn't how the game's supposed to be played. Every time you show up it's like there's a big black hole where my briefing's supposed to be and I'm getting sick of it. You Det. types might think you're above the law, but if I get one sniff of improper behaviour—'

'You'll turn around and walk away.'

'What?'

'You know the rules. Your lot and our lot don't mix. You want to know if I've killed anyone lately? Committed any light burglary? Of course you don't. You keep your noses out, maintain that comfortably plausible deniability and get to pretend that everything's whiter than fucking white. No pun intended.'

She threw the clipboard onto the bed and looked down at me. She knew I was right, and it obviously stung. I dropped my voice to something consolatory, even though she was bound to think of it as patronising.

'Go home, Penelope. Go back to Thames House and tell your boss that the smarmy bastard won't talk. Take the grief, go out, get drunk and forget all about it. Then go back to hunting terrorists your way and let me get on with it in mine. You know it makes sense.'

She turned around and walked out of the room without another word, leaving me to kick myself over the fact that she'd found out as much as she had. The other question was why I'd ended up in a military hospital. I was Captain Harris last time I'd been sent to train with the SAS, and Miss Marsh's comment about them being called out to get me made me wonder exactly what the hell had been going on.

My ignorance didn't last long. In about the time it would have taken Marsh to get out of the hospital car park, the Boss wandered in and sat down next to me.

'Fucked that up, didn't you?' His tone was mild, which probably meant that bollocking number two was about to arrive.

'Just a bit, sir.'

'Well, I'm not going to shout, but you need to get this fixed pretty bloody swiftish. If she's switched sides, then the Sisterhood won't just know that someone's after them, they'll know who. I don't need to explain the consequences of that to you, do I? Let alone what might happen if the word gets out. Bad enough that we exist as a rumour, but if that rumour ever gains substance, let alone someone willing to spill the beans, then we're all in trouble. So if your little fuck-up starts to spoil my day, I'll have no alternative but to defend myself and this Service. Am I clear?'

'Yes, sir.'

'Good. Now we're going to get you out of here and patch you up. Then it's back to work for you. Find these women, and stop them. No witnesses, no mess. Bring Annie back in so we can sort her head out, but I want nothing else left of these bitches. Understood?'

'Yes, sir.'

'Right, then.' He got up to leave.

'One question, sir.'

'Yes?'

'Marsh said that the SAS brought me in, and I'm registered under the name I used at Stirling Lines. I thought our own people would have been deployed.'

'They were, but this was the nearest facility and the only way you were getting in was as a soldier. Miss Marsh just fell for the illusion as she was supposed to.' Then he was gone, and three anonymous-looking blokes in paramedic uniforms came in. I recognised this bunch immediately: I knew them as 'The Hippies', a team of healers who seemed able to put you back together faster than an Essex joyrider could have it away with your BMW. I was loaded into a wheelchair, into the back of an ambulance, and as we pulled out of the hospital they grouped round me and started chanting. It only took about half an hour, and my nose was back where I usually kept it. Not only that, I felt as if I'd had a week off and come back with the energy of a bouncy six-year-old. Good shit, but it was one of the few things that still left me a little weirded out about the Service. Anywhere else, you get hurt and they give you time off, and right then I could have used a few days just to get my own head back together. At least they had clean clothes for me, which are always good for my morale.

The ambulance dropped me off by my car, exactly where I'd left it and in the same condition, so I got back in and drove the couple of miles round the corner to Pickerell House.

Chapter Fourteen

The house's isolation worked in our favour now the same way it had for the Sisterhood earlier. Somehow we'd managed to get a bunch of forensic guys in there without anyone noticing, which meant that there was no media irritation for me to avoid. I've had to do all sorts of rubbish to get into a place when there's a camera crew staking it out: from fake beards to full-on switching places inside a van with one of the crime scene guys in facemask and protective gear. Given what had gone down the previous night, I was very glad to be nothing more than an anonymous bloke that everyone seemed to assume was from Scotland Yard or something.

I showed my ID (Special Branch again) to the plod at the gate and drove up to park behind a van from the local nick, being careful to make sure my number plate wasn't visible from anywhere except directly behind it. It was a false plate, of course, but that doesn't stop a man from watching his back.

Hopping out of the car, I walked across the gravel and stepped over the threshold. There was a distinctly nasty air to the place, one that I'd noticed before but ignored while I was more worried about physical dangers. This time, though, I stopped to give it my full attention. Female energy gone nasty, it felt like. Not so much of the Kali but more like something twisted out of shape. I couldn't quite put my finger on it, but I didn't like it at all. Nor did the crew working the place, apparently: I could see unhappy faces all around, and not one person since the PC on the gate had a pleasant word to say. Something was definitely wrong, but all I could think of was a visit I'd paid to Jonestown back in the early nineties: not much of it left by then, but the air still had a *feeling* to it and none of the locals would go near the place.

Oh, bugger.

I turned to the nearest forensic: 'Are you checking for bodies?'

'No, sir, no indications that we should as of yet.'

'Start looking.'

'Sir?'

I stared at him, and he got the message. The message was 'Fuck off and do as you're told.'

So where to start? I decided on the separate stable block, since that had been a focus for some kind of ritual when I'd been watching them. I wandered across the gravel and took a look around the outside first. I hadn't really been expecting any external signs of particular interest, and my expectation proved correct. Nothing more than standard pagan protective glyphs around the window and door frames, the usual rubbish I'd expect to find anywhere there were witches to be found. To be honest, I was expecting the Sisterhood to be a little more imaginative. Never mind, though; it was time to check the door for nastiness and see if I could get it open.

A standard mortise lock: good, but less than a minute's work with the right tools and no pressure. The door opened into a single room decorated with drapes of dark-red velvet edged in gold. Expensive, good-quality stuff. Judging by the size of the place from the outside, those drapes were hiding something, and it turned out to be shelves of books and ritual kit. There were a number of spaces where things had obviously been grabbed in a hurry, and I was willing to bet that it was a selection of ritual knives, chalices and probably a sword. The book-shelves were well stocked with useful books, some of them pretty rare, but they didn't have anywhere near as many gaps as the kit shelves. I was inclined to guess that the Sisterhood had kept all their gear in this room rather than in the house, it being a sacred space and so on. Even though my mere presence defiled all that, I had to suppress a sudden urge to take a piss in the corner just to *really* fuck with it.

In the middle of the room were the remains of their ritual from the other night: a long table draped again with embroidered red velvet surrounded by five brass candlesticks about four feet high. The table was long enough for someone to lie on, which suggested a whole 'living altar' thing where one of the women would serve as a buffer between the ritual tools and the table. A pentagram was marked out on the floor with a candle-stick at each point of the star and symbols chalked around the edge between them. They looked familiar, but I'd have to check the books to be sure about what they were for. Definitely some kind of binding in there, though, but not demonic: there was no space marked out for anything to be summoned into. Interesting. I pulled a camera out of my pocket and started taking reference pictures to make my research easier later on.

As I walked around the room, something felt wrong. Some kind of dimensional weirdness, as though it was the wrong size inside compared with outside. I checked the depth of the shelves and paced the open area out, then went back outside and paced the perimeter. I did a few sums, added in the apparent thickness of the walls and came up with an answer. There was a crime scene geek hanging around, presumably wanting to come inside with me, so I asked him to provide the kind of help I needed.

'Don't s'pose you've got a fire axe knocking around, have you?'

'Umm, no, sir.'

'Sledgehammer, perhaps?'

'Not really something we use, sir.' He thought for a second. 'But the raid team used an Enforcer to get through the front door.'

I grinned. 'That'll do. Be a good lad and go fetch it for me, would you?'

A couple of minutes later, I was holding the animal in question: an Enforcer. Basically it's a long tube with a weight inside that slides back and forth and a couple of handles on each side. It's the gross alternative to lock picks, and can turn the average front door into matchwood pretty bloody quickly. I took it back inside, referred to my notes and started emptying the bookshelves at one end of the room. Next it was time for subtlety: a gentle knock on the back panel of each shelf until I found what I was looking for. It was at the opposite end from which I'd started (of course). After that it was just a matter of physics, and a couple of playful taps with the Enforcer revealed the secret door I'd suspected. That's 'revealed' as in 'fucked it so hard it wasn't much use for anything but kindling any more'. I also found the opening mechanism, a cunningly concealed switch, in bits on the floor afterwards. It would have been much cooler to have found it and made the door swing open like in some kind of movie, but I really didn't have the inclination to fart around like that and I was very much in the mood to hit stuff. The way things had gone over the last couple of days had thoroughly depleted my sense of humour and a little bit of therapeutic violence every so often doesn't do any harm.

Behind the door was a flight of bare stone steps going down. A convenient light switch showed me that it descended about twenty feet, ran the full width of the building and ended at a door heading back underneath the room up top. I pulled a torch from my pocket, a gun from my holster and a smile from nowhere in particular: it was about time I started seeing some of the Sisterhood's secrets, and I had a feeling this was going to be one of them.

Down the stairs.

The door was old metal-bound oak, like you'd find in a dungeon in a cheesy swashbuckler film. The Enforcer was going to have trouble with this one, so I was pleased to discover that it wasn't locked. Strangely, the lock seemed to be a bolt on my side that twisted to bar the door on both sides with the turn of a handle in the middle. Very melodramatic, very ritualistic. Obviously they were big on psychodrama in their methods. I slowly pulled the door open into the stairwell as best I could without trapping myself behind it or providing too much of a silhouette for anyone who might have been inside to aim at, then turned on my torch, crossed my wrists so the gun and torch shone next to each other (meaning that if a thing was lit it was in my sights) and stepped forward into pitch darkness to see what I could find.

From first impressions, it was another curtained room, only this time the curtains were black. Light was provided by a group of candles in each corner, and chains hung to each corner from the ceiling, with a couple more dangling over attachment rings in the floor. It was silent, and I didn't like the place one bit. Stretching my senses out, feeling for any other presences in the area, gave me nothing but the most intense Jonestown vibe I'd had yet. Whatever had happened to give me the heebie-jeebies had probably happened here. Time to look behind the drapes again.

What I found was not what I'd expected to find: everything you'd need to keep a Cabinet minister happy for months. There were straps, clips, harnesses and a selection of dildos, vibrators, gags and plugs for every orifice. I also found several pieces of machinery that obviously connected to the collection of toys and a couple of restraining rigs including one that reminded me a little too closely of the chair I'd had poor Jennifer McNair strapped into back at the interrogation suite a few days beforehand. Finally there were doors, thick and soundproof. The first one led into a largish room with a big white tank in the middle. A door on top showed me the contents: it was about half-full of slightly iffy-smelling water. I'd need to get that analysed by the science guys once I let them in to start poking about. No curtains in there, though. Nothing but the tank and only one door back into the main room.

The other door led into a changing room. There were

black silk robes there, sheer enough to be translucent, and a variety of interestingly small and tight garments in black leather and latex. Apparently the inner circle's proceedings were a lot more entertaining than the outer-circle stuff Annie had reported on before her promotion. That room was also draped in black, and I found yet another door behind one of the drapes. What the hell was going to be next?

An office wasn't quite what I'd expected, let alone one decorated with Scandinavian flat-pack furniture and designer lighting. Spend enough time with the bizarre and the banal becomes weird, and I allowed myself a brief second of culture shock. There were bookshelves again, but instead of magic tomes these held mainly psychology textbooks. There was also a good selection of material on interrogation, torture and brainwashing – including several books I recognised and a few I'd read myself. Nasty stuff.

I'd found something major here: Caroline's place of work. Candace Alder's extension of her work for the CIA. The means by which the Sisterhood had crawled under Annie's skin and into her head.

Another shelf held a collection of box files, each with a different name, each one a member of the Sisterhood – inner and outer circles. She'd obviously worked on them all, and one of the files bore Annie's name.

I took the file to the desk and opened it up.

Annie's whole life was in there – at least, the one that had been created for her as a cover. From birth certificate to employment history. Lovers, friends and all her secrets. All her secrets except one: there was no mention of the

Service. Somehow she'd kept that from them so far, and I'd need to ask the shrinks about that. There were a bunch of DVDs in there as well, each marked with Annie's name and a date. All but one of the dates were before Annie's promotion, but they stretched back over the last year. Candace liked to get her claws in early and keep them there.

I put Annie's file aside and started looking at the others. Each told a similar story: psychoactive drugs in various combinations, time in what was obviously a sensory-deprivation tank in the other room and something referred to as 'Treatment'. The treatment sessions were apparently recorded on the disks, or at least that's how the notes read. In each case, the progress of the member into unswerving obedience and submission was catalogued in Candace's neat handwriting, the dispassionate language making it all the more unpleasant to read. It's not often I come across someone even more fucked-up than I am, but this was definitely one of those times. But if every member of the Sisterhood had been through this, it meant that all of them were potential problems just waiting for orders.

I made a list of names and addresses, then picked up Annie's file and headed back upstairs. As I passed the file shelf I noticed a disk case marked 'Programs', and decided to grab it for good measure.

Returning to the outside world, I was surprised to discover late afternoon had arrived without my noticing; I'd been down there longer than I thought. I found the inspector in charge of the science show and handed him my list.

'These women: have them arrested immediately.'

'On what charge?' He was looking down his nose at me. He obviously didn't appreciate having all this bullshit on a Saturday, and clearly didn't like the fact that I wasn't kissing his arse the way everybody else seemed to be.

'What do I care? Use the fucking Prevention of Terrorism Act or something!'

'I can't just have a dozen women arrested because you say so!'

My sense of humour failure was clearly still ongoing, since the next second saw me holding the dickhead up against a wall by his throat. 'Listen, Sunshine. You do as you're fucking well told or I'll make sure you're transferred somewhere so fucking unpleasant you'll think *The Wicker Man* has a happy fucking ending! You understand me?'

'Yes.' He choked around my grip. Since we had an understanding, I let him go.

'Right, now fuck off and do as you're told. I want the lot of them in cells before sunset, and nobody talks to them. Go on, then!'

He was on his mobile phone as I got into the car and started back for the unit.

I may not have been about to watch normal TV, but that didn't stop me from grabbing something to eat on my way back and laying it out in front of me before I hit 'Play'.

I very quickly wished I hadn't.

The first shot was recognisable as Karen's bedroom. The accompanying notes listed what was rolling through Annie's bloodstream: a little cocktail of aphrodisiacs and hallucinogens just strong enough to ramp up her libido and shoot down her good sense. Just right for making her suggestible, too. It had been washed down with champagne and both parties were obviously feeling pretty frisky. I fast-wound through the sex: there were toys, and Annie ended up handcuffed to the bed for a while. She didn't seem too sure at first, but some smooth talking combined with the pharmaceutical cocktail had her playing along pretty quickly and by the end any initial difficulties she might have had didn't seem to be bothering her any more.

Two weeks later she was tied to the bed while Karen and another woman snorted coke off her tits, and begging to be given some, too.

Two more weeks, and she was taking care of three guys at once, while Karen rode another's face and gave the orders.

Another two weeks and I'd lost my appetite, pushing food aside and reaching for a bottle. It looked to me like Annie's dignity wasn't invited to play by then.

Maybe that was why Annie had fingered Karen for me to kill: she knew she'd been set up and it was the only way she'd have a chance of revenge. Hell hath no fury like an intelligence officer who knows you've fucked with her head. But why had she not mentioned any of it? Had she been conditioned not to talk about it or was she just embarrassed? Either way, she was going to have to answer a few questions before this mess was over.

The scene then switched to the underground room at Pickerell House. Annie tied to some kind of frame, with a vibrator strapped into position between her legs, being forced to orgasm over and over again. The notes said she'd spent twenty-four hours in sensory deprivation before that, been sedated and then woken up to find herself already in position. She'd been drugged again, of course, and the 'treatment' went on until she'd passed out for the third time.

Further downhill: Annie begging to be violated in every way possible. Machines, toys, fingers and even entire hands wherever someone decided to put them. She drank urine, played with shit and generally sank as low as she could before yet another degradation was found for her.

All the while, there were sessions in the tank followed by forced orgasm with suggestions being played to her through headphones. The human mind is pretty vulnerable during and after orgasm, and Candace was using that weakness to remould Annie the way she wanted. Eventually, things got even weirder, as Annie was taught to recite phrases in Latin as she came over and over again. From brainwashing to sex magic, Annie was being taught to be a battery for ritual power, her orgasms destined to provide magical energy for whatever purpose Hamilton and Alder had in mind.

The last session had her begging to be used, knowing what she was for, kissing Candace's feet and asking for stuff that turned my stomach. I couldn't watch any more, and the bottle was almost empty.

I threw the last of the Scotch down my neck and headed for bed, not sure if I was going to get any sleep. The footage had left me feeling seriously screwed up, and I needed oblivion in the hope that I might wake up in a fit state to find the bitches that had done this.

What had really fucked me up, though, wasn't on the

screen at all. The worst part was the semi-erect dick in my trousers, and the worry that a cold shower wasn't going to work and I'd need a wank before I could get to sleep.

Chapter Fifteen

I woke with a hangover, but that was only to be expected after half a pasty, a few chips and a bottle of Scotch. The footage I'd watched hadn't exactly helped my mood either, and had brought me to the conclusion that I'd want to kill Alder and Hamilton even if I hadn't been ordered to. Alder might be the mindfucking expert, but it was still Hamilton apparently giving the orders, so both of them were very firmly for the chop. It's not uncommon for me to be told to bring people in to see if there's a use for them, just as the Americans did with Nazi rocket scientists after the Second World War, so I was grateful there wouldn't be any of that bullshit this time.

I made coffee and sat down with my notes again, but nothing new surfaced. It was still the story of a ruthless process to break Annie's mind and turn her into nothing more than a battery. If this process was standard, then it was probably how Hamilton planned to power her ritual. Five women coming their brains out constantly, one at each point of the pentagram, would give out an awful lot of energy for Hamilton to direct as she saw fit; possibly even enough to break through the defences we kept running around the PM and royal family as a matter of course. With two members dead, Hamilton still had seven people: one for each point and two (herself and Alder, no doubt) to perform the actual ritual. I hated having to include Annie in the enemy's strength, but it was pretty clear that I had no alternative if only because she didn't have one. Assuming I was right, that meant Hamilton was still in business.

When I fired up the computer there was a message waiting for me, with a report attached. A murder, without any weirdness. That in itself was odd. Single male victim, in his mid-thirties, killed by a single shot to the head, with a follow-up to the heart and three completely gratuitous shots to the groin. Not my line at all. What made it relevant was the victim's job: Scotland Yard, Government Protection Team. Dickless was one of the Prime Minister's bodyguards.

All right, I thought, I'll play. I had sod all to go on until Temple Cloud turned up something useful, or we got another lead, so I decided that approaching the assassination from a more mundane angle might lead me back towards the Sisterhood in a way they might not be expecting. It was that or busting out the pendulum and trying to dowse for the bitches, and somehow I thought they'd have done something to prevent that.

Obviously the Boss agreed with me, since the message ended with an order to get over there and have a look.

Detective Sergeant Bob Fuller had died in bed, in his flat on the western outskirts of London. None of his neighbours had heard anything after he turned the stereo off just before midnight, except the downstairs neighbour who had heard his headboard banging on the wall after that. Someone had left the flat at about three in the morning, and that was believed to be his girlfriend of several months. Naturally, nobody knew her name, although she was described as a slim redhead. Fingerprints had already been taken and were being analysed as I was reading the report that brought me up to speed at his local police station. It was quite a pleasant change to have the plod being cooperative, but this time I was someone sent to help find a cop-killer. That sort of thing is generally discouraged by the police, for obvious reasons, and the amount of effort that was being swung into play for the late DS Fuller let me slip in with surprising ease.

It looked like sex was a theme here again, which would certainly have tied in with the Sisterhood's preferred methodology. The problem there was that the only slim redhead in the group had left the list of suspects two nights previously when I slit her throat as she slept in Pickerell House. That didn't stop this from being related, though. It was known that the Sisterhood was working with another group, and the death of one of the target's guards a week and a half before the planned date of the hit was too much of a coincidence. There are people, especially magicians, who don't believe in coincidences, but I'm not one of them; this just didn't feel like one. Since the second group wouldn't know that we were after the Sisterhood, they would have expected this to be written off as a crime of passion rather than a deliberate tying up of loose ends.

This gave me one major edge, and I planned to use it. Highly trained magicians can be pretty good at avoiding detection, especially detection via magic. Politically motivated weirdos with guns, however, are an absolute doddle. All I needed was a little privacy and a map. There was an atlas in the car, and the Service had a safe house not too far away that I could use without having to waste time on all that space-clearing bollocks.

Trouble was, I appeared to have developed a bit of a growth. I'd spotted an anonymous-looking white guy in casual clothes once too often, and his attempts to change appearance slightly every so often hadn't quite been good enough to fool me. But what to do with him? I checked the time, grinned evilly and headed for the East End, where I knew the perfect place to get the situation back under control.

East London has any number of charms: narrow streets that can confuse the hell out of you, large scary men who'll beat people up for a fee and perfectly respectable pubs that just happen to have young ladies taking their clothes off during the lunch hour being among them. It was to the last of these that I went. The Mitre was close enough to the City for a bloke to get up there, have a pint and an ogle and be back at the office before the end of his lunch break, and this was how Steve the landlord made an awful lot of his money. He did a bit of trade in dodgy goods from the back room as well, but it was generally considered rude to mention that. He was a useful bloke to know if you needed a gun in a hurry, or a DVD player, or pretty much anything else, really – nothing weird, though, and he just had me filed as a nondescript who occasionally wanted something quietly and without any fuss.

I parked up with some difficulty and headed in, making sure my tail could see where I was going. As luck would have it, Steve was behind the bar. It only needed thirty seconds and a twenty-pound note to get what I wanted, and by the time my new friend had caught up I was sitting at the bar with a pint of Steve's cheapest and nastiest lager, giving the impression of a man who was waiting for someone. That didn't take much work, since that was in fact exactly what I was doing.

About five minutes and half a pint of cheap lager later, the jukebox kicked off with something that might have been mistaken for sexy by a deaf man, and a girl in her early twenties walked into the middle of the bar. She was an all-right looker, and moved pretty well – a lot of the girls doing this sort of thing are actually proper dancers trying to earn a few extra quid on the side to cover the bills – and was dressed in cheap lingerie just the right side of tacky. All eyes moved to her, including mine but excluding my friend's. He was just that little bit too focused on me, so he didn't notice the girl dancing over to him until she started waving her arse in his face as she peeled off her pants. The look on his face was a picture, and only improved by his being unable to get clear as I slid off my barstool and headed out the side door.

It took him a good minute and a half to come out behind me, looking left and right for any sign of where I'd gone. Seeing no trace, he reached into his pocket and pulled out a mobile phone. His half of the conversation sounded unhappy, and I got the impression that he was being ordered back to base to wait until I was spotted by his colleagues. He hung up and wandered over to where my car was parked.

If the look on his face was a picture when I slipped out of the pub, you should have seen it when I stepped out of a doorway and punched his lights out. It was a good thing that my car had a decent-sized boot.

The safe house was one of those nice suburban joints with an attached garage, so I didn't have any trouble getting matey out of the boot and into the front room without being seen. By the time he woke up he was attached to a dining room chair with cable ties, and the table had been fitted out with the results of a quick scavenge. Oddly enough, we don't actually keep serious interrogation gear in every house. I suppose it's to prevent them from being blown if some smartarse burglar actually manages to get into one or something similar. But that's beside the point, since pretty much any house can provide enough kit to do the job if you know what you're doing.

Matey's first view, then, was a dining room not unlike any other you'd find in a nice middle-class suburb. The table was a little different, though: several kitchen knives, a couple of sets of pliers, a hammer, a big hammer and a power drill were laid out on top of a tea towel on the dining table, along with a sewing kit, some lemon juice, a container of salt, one of those big display candles, a tube of superglue and a roll of gaffer tape. Believe me, that was enough to get his attention. Obviously our boy knew his stuff, because he didn't look too comfortable when he saw me sitting alongside all this drinking a cup of tea. He drew breath to speak, so I cut him off.

'Didn't your mum ever tell you it's rude to follow people?'

'Buddy, you got no idea how much trouble you're in.' American accent, somewhere just south of Chicago at a guess. 'My people know where I am, and they'll have the cops here any minute.'

'I'd best be getting on then,' I replied calmly, and picked up the smaller of the two hammers. It had a nice rounded head that can work wonders on small joints like the fingers. His eyes widened: he was obviously expecting me to ask questions before I started hitting him. Then he got himself under control and braced for the oncoming pain. I laughed and put the hammer down. 'Sorry, mate, but your mobile's in a bin far away from here and the police aren't going to come anywhere near this place. You've fallen right down the rabbit hole, and the only way back out is through my good offices. Either you tell me what's going on and we discuss it, or you vanish. I'll give you some time to think about it.'

I got up, went out to the kitchen, found some food in the fridge and made myself a fry-up. I was starving, and it was a good way to give the guy some time to think. The human mind is a wonderful thing: it can come up with all sorts of stuff if you let it, and that was what I was allowing his to do. In the other room, my guest was looking at the tools laid out in front of him and trying to work out what I was going to do with them, so he could be prepared for it when it came. I knew this for a fact because I've been there myself, and it can be a lot worse than anything the interrogator actually does to you when he gets going. When there's time, you can mess with the sense of place and all that fun stuff the way I did with Jennifer, but time was pressing and this was as good a softening-up technique as I could manage under the circumstances. Food done, I went into the dining room to eat. I sat at the other end of the table, tucked in and paid absolutely no attention to what was opposite me. The food was good, and I must have really needed it since a pretty large plate of fried meat only seemed to last about thirty seconds.

Then it was back out into the kitchen to wash the plate and put it away. It's only polite to leave these places the way you'd like to find them, and I'd be really pissed off if I came in dragging an unconscious Yank to discover a pile of dirty dishes in the sink. Basic manners cost nothing, and I'd like to think my colleagues would extend me the same courtesy.

At last, with a fresh brew in my hand, I went back in to talk. The American wasn't looking happy: he'd seen me coolly ignore him all the way through lunch and was obviously convinced I was some kind of psycho. Personally I just think of myself as a professional, but I prefer to leave that particular brand of mumbo-jumbo to people who believe in it. I lit the candle and sat down facing my subject.

'So. What shall we talk about?'

'How about the depth of the shit you're in?'

Ah, bravado. He was going to tough it out. Obviously he didn't believe me about the lack of back-up.

'Right now, mate, I'm the one on the edge of the shit pit trying to throw you a rope before you need a snorkel. Who are you, and why were you following me?'

'Fuck you.'

I liked his tone – it was almost conversational rather than full of too much bluster. He was a little more than just some thug, obviously.

'Either you're a very silly American intelligence officer, or you're a dead man. Which is it?' The look on his face had already answered me before I finished the sentence. He'd hidden it well, but the slight twitch told me all I needed to know. 'Which flavour of spook, though? Will your embassy even admit you're one of theirs, or will they just take the story about a nasty car crash and leave it at that?'

'I have no idea what you're talking—'

'Don't insult my intelligence. Have you ever seen a kneecapping? The best way is to use a power drill, like this one –' I lifted it up to show him '– and drill through from the back. You'll never be able to bend your knee properly again, never be able to walk straight, and you can forget about running. Every time it rains your knee will hurt, and you'll remember just how stupid you were when you failed to identify yourself at the appropriate moment. I hate doing this shit when I don't have to, and once you make me start you'll have to really impress me before I stop. So let's have your identification protocols now, or I'll have to treat you as a hostile agent caught on foreign soil.'

Silence.

'Fair enough, then.' I looked at the assembled tools and considered my next move. If he was an American spook, then I'd catch more flak than I could probably handle if I hurt him badly. Trouble was, if I pussy-footed around he'd know it and I'd have no chance of cracking him. Things are always too bloody complicated when foreign governments get involved. If he was anything other than a bloody Yank I could have given him to Brutus for auctioning off, but

Brutus still has an affection for his countrymen even though he lives over here. It would have to be something painful but not permanently damaging. A fine line to walk.

Walk.

That was it.

I had his shoes and socks off quickly enough, then went to the garage for a piece of wood I'd noticed earlier. Beating the soles of the feet is a classic in the Far East, and hurts like all hell if it's done right. The best thing was that if I stopped before anything broke he ought to be able to get away without any long-term disability, just enough inconvenience that he'd remember to do the smart thing next time he got caught out in a friendly nation. Putting the wood down on the table, I lifted his feet and gaffer-taped them to the tabletop; not hugely secure, but a good way to start. I figured that after the first dozen or so strokes I'd stick him on his back with his feet in the air so I could get a really good chopping motion going. He watched all this with a mounting sense of unease. I think he'd convinced himself that there was no way I'd go through with it and this illusion was failing to survive my obviously businesslike manner. I raised the stick above my head and made a couple of experimental swings for targeting. The third swing hit him across both feet full force, and he screamed.

'Oh dear,' I said, 'that won't do, will it?' I was right, it wouldn't. Too much bloody noise might get the neighbours' attention and I really didn't need that, so I stuck his slightly fragrant socks in his mouth and covered it with gaffer tape. 'Another five, then you get the chance to answer questions, all right?'

I hit him again. He screamed like a good 'un and made me very glad I'd gagged him, so I hit him a third time.

Then my mobile phone started ringing. Not answering it wasn't really an option, so matey got an unscheduled break. They'd verified my guest's identity and he was indeed an American agent attached to the embassy. This news, to put it mildly, did not make my day. Quite the opposite, in fact, since he was going to be walking home with a limp now because he'd been too stupid to take advantage of his diplomatic immunity when I gave him the chance. I took notes from what I was told, promised not to hurt him any more and hung up.

When I got back he was doing his best to look defiant, with a fairly impressive degree of success. He took the removal of the gag with some interest, presumably wondering what I was going to do next. Whatever he was expecting, it wasn't this.

'James William Peterson the Third, you are a very stupid man.'

'I don't know what you're talking about.'

'Mister Peterson, you are an officer of the National Security Agency stationed at the American Embassy, where you nominally hold the position of an administration officer. You are also a total fucking moron for not telling me this and saving yourself what was about to be a very unpleasant afternoon.'

No reaction.

'Look,' I continued, 'you're an accredited diplomat, which means your fucking photograph is on file. All it took was a photo sent back to the office while you were out and a records search. Why the hell would you be so stupid as to follow me yourself?'

And then it hit me.

'Candace Alder.' Now that got a reaction. 'You're doing this yourself because you don't have anyone else cleared for it, aren't you? Bloody hell, when you Yanks screw something up, you really do screw it up, don't you?'

'So who are you?' he asked.

'That, my boy, is none of your business. All you need to know is that she's on my list, and you'd do well to stay out of it from here on in.'

'You can't touch her. She's protected.'

'Not from me she isn't.'

'You're not listening, asshole. She's *protected*. Immune. Not to be touched under any circumstances. My government says so, and so does yours. You should have seen that when you tried to check your records.'

'Which ones?'

'Whatever you call them, the police computer, why should I care?' Given that five minutes before I'd been warming up to torture him, he was bouncing back pretty well. Arrogant, sure, but there are times when I like that. I hadn't even untied him yet and he was starting to give the impression that he was in a position to throw his weight around. He was wrong.

'Your Ms Alder has been implicated in a terrorist action, sunshine. There's no way she's going to get away with that.'

'Bullshit.'

'Wrong answer. Hasn't it occurred to you that you

might be dealing with the big boys here? You think the plod are into taking people to quiet little houses and beating information out of them? They're not. People like me only happen when you do something to *really* piss Her Majesty off, when there's a credible threat and when we can't be arsed to fuck around with the niceties. Now, I'm supposed to send you on your way, but if I get a hint that you're still sniffing around I'm probably not going to waste any time on friendly little chats like this, I'll just fucking kill you and let the suits sort out an apology afterwards. All right?' No shouting, just a calm recitation of the facts.

'So tell me what's happening.'

I took a gamble and ran him through a very carefully edited version of the case: brainwashing, consorting with terrorists and the objective. I skipped the weird bits for his own sake, since that wouldn't exactly have sat too well with his impression of a standard issue (but nastier than average) national security type. He sat through it all, still tied to the chair, and was obviously disturbed by the tale.

'How can I confirm this?' he asked. It was a good question.

'I'll have someone contact you. Deal?'

'Deal.'

'Good. I suppose I'd better let you go, then.'

Once again he didn't see the punch coming. Luckily he didn't feel it when the chair fell over and he knocked the back of his head on the floor.

Chapter Sixteen

With the dumbass Yank dropped off on a bench in Regent's Park I returned to the safe house with the intention of getting back to work. I'd wasted an afternoon on the stupid bastard, and wasn't exactly happy about it. I was particularly unhappy that I'd not had a chance to explain to him just how unhappy I was, but apparently it damages international relations if we send back the representatives of our allies beaten to a bloody pulp. Whoever made that rule obviously never had to deal with the fuckers.

So it was in this spirit of joy that I set myself up ready to locate DS Fuller's bit of stuff. I'd liberated a used condom from the bathroom of his flat as a nice link both to him and to her, got my little copper pendulum out and spread a selection of maps out ready to help narrow things down as I worked in on her. I closed the curtains since it was starting to get dark, and I didn't exactly want the neighbours peering in to see what I was up to, then it was time to clear my mind, focus on the map and start dowsing.

Map one: the world. It wasn't a shock when I had her still in the UK, but better not to make any assumptions at this point. I could have spent two hours working over Britain for a trace and not got anywhere because she was in Calais buying a case of beer, so I always start with the bigger picture.

Map two: the British Isles. Somewhere in northern England. Narrowing it down over and over again, to county, then town, then neighbourhood, then street and finally to the house she was sitting in. I sent an email to the Boss, letting him know what I'd found out and what I proposed to do about it. I had a reply pretty swiftly, giving me the good news that I was going to get a lift.

The lift in question was by helicopter, and I was glad of a chance to rest up for the length of the trip. Helicopters are too noisy for actual kip but I've spent enough time practising meditation in all sorts of weird places and under conditions that made this look like a Zen garden, and a bit of time spent contemplating my navel did wonders for my temper, which was starting to fray a little at the edges.

Four hours later I was sitting in the back garden of my target's house, under an apple tree, wearing all the usual urban penetration gear and thinking invisible thoughts. Patience was the key: I wanted everyone asleep so I could just sneak in, drug whoever happened to be inside and throw missy in the back of a van for a little tête-à-tête. Sweet, simple and refreshingly free of bullshit; it would certainly make a change after the last week.

You might be wondering why we don't do this kind of location for every case that gets the plods' knickers in a twist, and I'll tell you. We're supposed to be a *secret*. People like me are in the business of keeping all this supernatural nonsense quiet, so the most you get to see is some bloke chasing ghosts on TV or Mrs Medium reading the tea-leaves. We don't want you to start messing around with this stuff, because if you've got everyone rolling around with this kind of capability you'll have anarchy in ten minutes flat. We're about maintaining the status quo. Keeping a lid on the world so it doesn't get out of hand. If the general population knew it was this easy we'd spend all our time refusing to look for lost cats and all the real bad guys would have a lot more freedom to act in all the random background noise. We like it this way and, even though you might think otherwise, believe me when I say *so do you.*

It was getting round to about three in the morning and I was starting to think about making my move when the fuck-up fairy came to play. A figure slipped quietly over the wall to my left and started making its way to the back door. I knew the police hadn't got a clue who or where this woman was, so it wasn't official. Which left bad guys as the only other option. Just my fucking luck.

I let the guy do a passable job of getting through the door locks before I took him. Nice and quiet, just stepped up behind him and hit him in a couple of strategic pressure points, then caught him as he went down to avoid noise. He was a heavy bugger, but I just about managed to hoist him over my shoulder quietly and get him round the outside of the house to park him in the back of the van. I was partly tempted to put him out of commission for good, but there was a little plan starting to kick off in the back of my head for which he might come in very handy indeed. My driver, a local named Colin, looked a bit surprised at the unexpected delivery but had the good sense to keep his gob shut. Then it was back round to the now-unlocked door, and in we go.

To be punched in the guts by someone in the kitchen. Fucking typical. I punched the guy on the point of the jaw even as I was doubling up from the impact, and he went straight onto his back. Seeing that he was out, I kicked him in the balls for good measure so he'd have something to think about when he woke up and then caught the front door opening out of the corner of my eye. Time to make a decision. I grabbed chummy and threw him over my shoulder, then it was straight to the door where I could see a female figure climbing into a car thirty feet away. Colin was on the ball and starting the van, so I opened the side door and piled in – my passenger still on my shoulder – with a shout of 'After her!'

And away we went. The back of a Transit van really isn't exactly the best place I can think of for enjoying a car chase, and while Colin was making all the smooth moves up front I was rolling around in the back with two unconscious blokes who'd both indicated a distinct interest in negatively affecting my sense of well-being. I just about managed to secure my second guest between corners, then attached each of them to opposite sides of the van. That had to be done first, just in case they decided to wake up and cause more trouble.

The van had a little hatch between the back and the driver's section, so I grabbed hold of a couple of loading straps and got myself into a roughly stable position, then gave it a knock with my forehead. When Colin opened up I could see that we were heading out of town and he was glued to the back of our target vehicle, a beaten-up VW with a 'Save the Whales' sticker in the back window.

'What do you want me to do, Boss?' Colin was a smart

boy – smart enough to do as he was told and not get clever, and smart enough to know when to ask for instructions. This was outside the plan, and he wasn't being paid to make any big decisions.

'Run her off the road.' I didn't really see any alternatives apart from waiting to see who ran out of fuel first.

'Right you are. Best hold on to something,' said Colin with a grin, and the van leapt forward with a scream of the engine. I held on to my straps like grim death as we shot out and around the VW, then Colin brought our nose straight across hers in the kind of graceful carve you normally only see on Hyde Park Corner. There wasn't much the poor bitch could do but swerve, and the trees by the side of the road were solid enough to catch her before she went much further.

Colin pulled in and I hopped out of the back while he kept the engine running. There was a chloroform pad in my pocket that had been intended for this young lady, and I put it to good use as she was groggily groping under the dashboard. She came out of the car easily enough, as did the gun she'd been reaching for, so it was handcuff time again and a place in the back of the van for her. More importantly, I got to sit in the front this time. The gun went into the glove compartment and Colin set course for London while I got some kip.

Having got rid of Colin in Watford I needed to find somewhere to park the van for a bit. I had a plan, but the general paranoia in central London made it tricky. It took me longer to sort than I wanted, but the car park by Turnham Green Tube Station would most likely do for the hour or so I'd need. Last thing to do was make sure my passengers all got a nice big injection of sedative just to make sure they didn't get noisy in my absence. All it would need to screw this up was one random copper deciding to take an interest, and they'd be getting plenty of attention soon enough.

Into the station, grab a Travelcard and on to the District Line for a couple of stops west. If my information was correct, I should just about make it in time.

I did, but with seconds to spare. Penelope Marsh was just opening the door of her flat.

'What the hell are you doing here?' It was a perfectly reasonable question. I shouldn't have known where she lived, but she took the shock of her work life intruding on home turf pretty well, considering it was only about seven o'clock in the morning.

'Good morning, Miss Marsh. Got time for a chat?' That grabbed her attention.

'What about?'

'A little something you might like to know. You wanted information and now I can do you a swap.'

'What have you got?' Her voice was suspicious now, torn between a desire to know and reasonable concern about my motives. She didn't like the idea that I'd come to her front door rather than going through channels, and to be honest I didn't blame her one bit; if she'd shown up at mine I'd probably have killed her. I stepped inside her flat and she led me to the front room. It looked more like a safe house than somebody's home, but some people like to live like that.

'Did you hear about the PM's guard who got himself killed?'

'Ye-es . . .'

'What would you do if I told you where the main suspect was, along with a couple of friends?'

'I'd wonder what the hell it had to do with you.'

'Good answer.' I smiled, which seemed to unsettle her even more. 'What if I then said you can have the credit for the collar?'

'I'd wonder what the hell you want in return.'

'Everything you get out of the interrogation.'

'I can't do that.'

'Then they'll never be seen again. My way you get loads of brownie points with your bosses, Special Branch will love you and MI5 get to look to the outside world like they're doing something useful. Word is that you're trying to get transferred to fieldwork. Well, this won't do you any harm with that, will it?'

'And all you want is the results of the interrogation.'

'I want copies of the tapes and transcripts, unedited. Nothing else.'

'Fine, but only if the info's good and they haven't escaped by the time I get there.'

'Deal.'

'So, where are they?'

'In the back of a van in Chiswick.' I threw her the keys, wrapped in a piece of paper that had the exact location of the van, along with its description and registration number. She looked at me as if I'd just told her I was really a woman, and shown her my tits to prove it – I thought I'd have to pick her jaw up off the ground for her. 'Don't ask how they got there, just enjoy the results of a nice clean collar and an outstanding piece of detective work by the Security Service.'

'You have got to be kidding me.'

'About the detective work? Yeah. Just relax and enjoy the benefits. But don't forget the deal.'

'And how do I get this information to you, exactly?'

I stood up and made my way towards the door. 'Shouldn't worry about that, Penny. I'll find you.' Then it was out the door and away before she had time to come up with a clever reply.

Chapter Seventeen

I have to admit that I was feeling better for the preceding day's violence. Things had not been going the way I wanted, and sometimes there's nothing better than kicking some poor bastard in the bollocks to deal with the frustration. I was also feeling pretty good about the stunt I'd pulled on Miss Marsh, so it was just the bad guys who were getting up my nose. Marsh now owed me big time, and she knew it. The payback she'd get in respect and good relations with the police would work wonders for her reputation inside MI5, and it was all a gift from me. That was going to come in handy one day, I was sure of it.

But for the moment I really had nothing to do. There would be a delay while I waited for the interrogators to work their own special magic on last night's catch, and the rest of it was waiting for a fresh lead. I decided to do something that would make the Boss happy, and file a report. Not only would it keep Him Upstairs in touch with what was happening out here in the real world, it was a good way to get my thoughts in order. I sat down in a small pub with my laptop and started typing, laying out the sequence of events as they'd happened while looking for details I might have missed. One thing struck me: I'd been pretty bloody unlucky quite a few times, and only pulled off a lot of stuff by the skin of my teeth. But this had only been the case when dealing with the bad guys; everything with the authorities had gone as planned. That was interesting. If I didn't know better I'd say I'd been cursed ...

But I didn't, not this time. With Annie on side the Sisterhood might have found a way to mojo around with my luck, and that *would* explain all the fun I'd been having with people getting away and the poor timing. It was definitely worth taking a look at, if only to exclude the worry. Things were going to get nasty before the case was wrapped up, and the last thing I needed was any niggling doubts when I got back on their scent.

It was mid-afternoon by the time I encrypted the report and sent it off through the pub's wi-fi connection. I'd washed some lunch down with a couple of lemonades and was in pretty good nick, all things considered. The TV news was reporting that a break in the investigation of DS Fuller's murder was considered imminent, which meant that somebody must have started talking. The PM was there, too, spouting the usual oh-so-sincere bullshit that comes out every time someone in uniform dies unnaturally. I had no illusions that I'd get the same treatment: I've got no living relatives to lie to, so I'll probably end up being stuck in a crematorium sometime after hours. Quick, quiet and as little fuss as possible – which suits me down to the ground. Might as well go out the same way I lived, eh?

I had no plans to get in a box any time soon, however, so thought it was worth checking out my luck. I started making use of the internet to look at my options, and thought about putting together a list of potential candidates to help me out. In half an hour I went through a dozen different gods, all basically facets of the same essential thing, plus a pile of other entities from the places that hang on the edge of our dimension. I had to make a choice between something small and easy to handle that might not be able to deal with a hex if there was one, and a larger, less controllable entity that might try having a pop at me if something went wrong. Caution won out, since if my luck was being fucked with it would be the perfect time for stuff like that to go pear-shaped.

So with all that in mind, I decided to ask an old friend. I'd first met Geoff in training when I joined the Service, the only point in our careers when we spend any real time with our colleagues. He was a good bloke: solid, dependable and methodical. If he lacked anything it was an ability to improvise, which is why he'd had so much trouble defusing the bomb that had taken both his legs and a chunk of his torso off a few years back. But even now he could be a useful sort to know: he was in a better position than me to spot all kinds of nonsense, and this was the sort of situation where I could make good use of that ability.

Geoff hung out in Kensal Green, and wouldn't be available to talk until after dark. I decamped to a more modern pub just across the road from his place and waited till about half an hour before sundown, then quietly wandered in before they started thinking about shutting the huge wrought-iron gates. I found a nice, quiet bench to sit on and thought invisible thoughts while the groundskeeper-types walked straight past me on their security checks.

After a couple of hours freezing my arse off, it looked all clear: the sun was down and the staff had found somewhere better to be. I wandered over towards Geoff's place, found his nameplate and gave him a quiet knock.

'Geoff, you in, mate?' There was no response so I tried again, only a little louder: still nothing. 'Bloody hell, Geoff, do you want me to die of hypothermia out here or what?'

'Might be an idea – I could use the company,' Geoff said as he stepped halfway out of the shadows. 'What do you want, anyway?'

'What makes you think I want something? I could have just—'

'Spare me. I can see right through the bullshit anyway, easy as you can see through me.' He waved a spectral hand in front of my face to illustrate the point. 'Now what was it you wanted? You're not exactly one to hang out in graveyards at night for no reason. Probably afraid of running into a few of your previous customers.'

'Am I being fucked with?' When Geoff's in a mood like this it's easier just to get on with things. 'Luck, timing, anything like that?'

'No, mate.' Geoff laughed. His laugh hadn't exactly been the most infectious when he'd been alive, but these days it's not a pleasant noise and a slight shiver went down my spine. 'The only person fucking with you is yourself. Too much guilt, too much second-guessing and too much worrying about doing the right thing. Just do your job, yeah? Leave the conscience at home and do what you have to, or you'll be in here with me and that'll spoil the tone something rotten.'

'Yeah, right. Given who you're parked next to I wouldn't talk so much about tone.' Geoff's next-door neighbour had been a bit of a naughty boy in Africa before he retired, and had met his fate at the end of a machete several years later after things had quietened down. Geoff looked at me for an extra second, then raised an eyebrow.

'You're not messing around with the cult of Azathoth, are you? You've got a funny whiff about you – primal chaos sort of thing.'

'Not that I'd noticed.'

'Well, I'd bloody well notice if I were you, Sunshine. You never know what that kind of chaos type will be up to next. Anyway, I'm off to watch Goths shagging – you can tag along if you like.'

'No thanks, mate, I'd best be getting on.'

'Your loss. There's this one girl who's a regular up here: looks like butter wouldn't melt, but stick a slab of marble under her and the things she does ... I tell you, if I still had a dick it would be up all night watching her!'

'Whatever works for you, mate. Thanks for the help.'

'No problem, but would it kill you to visit when you're not up to your arse in crap? Maybe leave me some flowers or something? Just because I haven't got a pulse any more doesn't mean I wouldn't mind a little company, y'know?'

'All right, I'll drop by and watch Goths with you one night when I've wrapped this one up. How does that sound?'

'I'll believe it when I see it. But bring a robe if you do, they seem to like that.' What that was supposed to mean

I didn't want to think about, so I let him head off into the graveyard as I made my way to the fresh hole in the fence that this evening's lovers had made.

Geoff's comment about the cult of Azathoth got me thinking on my way back to the safe house. I'd been trying to work out exactly what the Sisterhood's motives were since Annie had given me the news, and frankly none of it made sense. Unless something much bigger was afoot, all killing the PM would do would be to put the nation in a state of shock (and possibly gratitude in some quarters) and throw the government into some temporary disarray while his replacement was found. Useful if you were planning a coup, but there was no way that Hamilton or Alder had those sorts of resources, and it was bloody unlikely that any terrorist group they could find would either. My only real idea was that they were contracting their services out to the terrorists to help them make a point, but I wasn't sure about how that theory fitted with the women's profiles. Maybe there was some revenge in there as well, but what if it was just a matter of stirring the shit for its own sake? That would fit with a chaos cultist pretty well ...

You see, there are two types of chaos people. There are the magicians, who are the type that are seen in public and range from leather-trenchcoat-wearing wannabes to smart, flexible people who hop between systems and methods in much the same way that I do; and then there are the cultists, who are scary weirdos who just want to fuck things up because it gets their gods off. I was pretty sure that the Sisterhood didn't fit into type one, but if Hamilton and Alder were helping with this because of the mayhem it would bring about then it might well put them into type two. The use of sex to turn their followers into gibbering sacks of drool would fit with that as well – removing all chance of rational thought while they were in an altered state of consciousness for rituals. I hadn't seen a copy of the *Necronomicon* at Pickerell House, but that didn't mean they didn't have one knocking around – or that they needed one at all, since there are plenty of less famous books that will twist your brain inside out if you give them the chance. Their ritual kit would have given me more information, but they'd taken that with them, of course. Just another theory to add to the mix until I managed to get my hands on some hard data.

The sun was pushing itself over the horizon when I got back to base, making it later than I'd thought. Time always goes a bit funny when I visit Geoff, which isn't a surprise when you remember that he's operating on a slightly different level from the rest of us, and I took one look at the bed and fell onto it already snoring.

By the time I crawled out of bed at lunchtime the news was full of captured terrorists. Turns out my little trio had quite a rep in the international blowing-stuff-up community and there was a bit of a queue waiting impatiently to talk to them about misbehaviour from Belfast to Berlin and several points beyond. Special Branch and the Anti-Terrorist Squad were sitting in front of news conferences looking very pleased with themselves and crediting teamwork and suchlike while trying to slap themselves and each other on the back. It was perfect, better than I'd hoped, in fact. I was willing to bet that this was the sort of thing that would get little Penny Marsh onto the fast track straight to where I could make good use of her, and her name would be so wrapped up with this that the truth escaping would ruin her. Served her right for asking me to help her out, really.

More importantly for me, if the plod were admitting that these three were in custody it meant that somebody had spilled enough to MI5 that they were willing to hand them over for legitimate justice. That meant that it was time to make Miss Marsh's transition complete by getting her to hand over the details, and hopefully tell me what was happening behind the doors of her own agency. Once she'd done that I'd own her.

She was being bought lunch in a rather nice restaurant by a couple of older men in suits when I found her. Catching her eye wasn't a problem, and she excused herself as soon as the conversation gave her a chance. As our paths crossed for a second, her ostensibly on the way to the toilet and me on the way out, I whispered, 'I want it tonight,' and named a pub in Covent Garden that would be busy enough to hide our little transaction. We were past each other before she had a chance to reply, but she looked as if she knew she didn't have a choice.

I spent the next few hours in the British Library catching up on the cult of Azathoth. To cut a long story short, they were the sort of loonies who think that civilisation is weird and unnatural, and want to bring the whole thing crashing down to return things to what they consider to be their natural state. Completely barking, of course. There were a few guarded references to occasional groups who looked as if they might have come across one of my predecessors if you read between the lines, and I took a little hope from that: if we'd had them before then there was a good chance that I could take them again. I took notes on rituals, important dates and totems, and spotted that they had an affinity for rituals on the full moon. Again, that added up. I didn't exactly have a ton of evidence to back up a conclusion, but enough data fitted the model to keep it in play as a possibility. Maybe I'd find out more from the MI5 file.

Miss Marsh was already waiting when I got to the pub, sipping a gin and tonic and fending off the occasional clumsy attempt to chat her up. I hung back in the crowd for a few minutes, checking about to see if she'd brought friends. I didn't discount the possibility that she might have decided to be straight with her bosses and that this was a set-up, with her aiming for bonus points by handing me over. That would have been messy but resolvable in time, but time wasn't a luxury I had. The full moon was only eight days away, and I was already unhappy about the pace at which I was moving. If I'd had to get the Boss to pull me out of custody he would have hit the roof, and I wouldn't have blamed him for denying all knowledge and letting me rot in an asylum somewhere, or arranging for me to have a fatal run-in with a fellow prisoner. As far as I could tell everything looked all right, and a quick scan of the room on the other level didn't reveal anyone paying too much attention to Miss Marsh on anything other than a purely sexual basis.

I worked my way to the table in such a way that she didn't notice me until I was standing in front of her, despite the pretty close watch she was keeping on things. I think the suit helped, since she'd never seen me in one before. I gave her my very best smile and asked if I could join her, and she graciously waved to the stool opposite her.

'Good evening, Miss Marsh. Shall we pretend that I'm chatting you up? It gives you a nice excuse to blow me off when we're done.'

'Fine. I don't suppose you're about to tell me what's going on, are you? At least I know the PM's involved now. We'll have to warn him, of course.'

'That was the plan,' I lied. 'Now what do you have for me?'

'Why can't you just—' I raised my eyebrows and smiled at her. 'Fine, keep your secrets. The woman talked once we let her know who else we had. Turns out that one was her boyfriend, her real boyfriend, and the other was halfway through breaking in to knock them off before you interrupted him. Apparently they didn't want any loose ends.'

'How very efficient. What format?'

'Three DVDs.'

'Talkative, was she? Why don't you just drop them into the top of my briefcase? That's lovely.' I almost didn't see her do it, and I was watching. 'Now, would you like to find me immensely dull, or would you prefer to be waiting for your boyfriend? Which have you been using on the Casanova squad?'

'You know I'll find out who you are the end, don't you?'

'I think you can devote your energies more effectively somewhere else.'

'Was that a warning?' She was arching an eyebrow at me, trying to read the subtext.

'An opinion.' It *was* a warning, but I preferred at least to try to keep things civil. I didn't want to alienate her, after all.

'Then I think I find you very dull indeed. Goodnight.' She stood up without finishing her drink and walked straight out. I checked the room to see who watched her go, and caught a couple of commiserating looks from the other failures. No undue interest as far as I could tell, so maybe she was playing straight with me. I wasn't overly worried about her threat to find out more about me since I knew she didn't have enough clearance to get near my fake Army or police records – let alone anything else. If she needed a hobby, she'd be better off taking up knitting.

Chapter Eighteen

I decided that it was time to head back to the industrial unit outside of Bath for a bit, as a little distance from all the interest in me would hopefully give it time to calm down. Too many questions still didn't have answers and I didn't want anyone interrupting me while I tried to work out what at least one or two of those answers were. One thing needed doing before I left town, and that was the American. He'd had a couple of days to think things over and the chapter and verse I'd had when he was identified included his home address. I decided to pay him a visit.

By the time he got home, I was sitting on his sofa reading a book on conspiracy theories and sniggering at all the bits the author had got wrong. He probably did the same thing, come to think of it; you take the laughs where you can in this game. He won the prize for unflappability by going straight to the fridge for a beer and offering me one while he was there.

'No thanks, mate,' I replied, 'I'm driving. I won't stay long anyway.'

'Whatever.' He shrugged. 'Just trying to be hospitable.' It was likely that he was probably trying to get a sample of my DNA and fingerprints, but it would have been rude to say so openly.

'I thought I'd do you the courtesy of warning you off.

Alder's a dead woman, no matter what your people have to say.'

'Well, that's real neighbourly of you, but my people say "Go ahead".'

'Oh?'

'Part of the deal is that she stays out of trouble and from what you told me she hasn't. That makes her fair game as far as we're concerned, so if you guys need to take care of her, we're not going to stop you.'

That was a pleasant surprise. I'd expected an argument about it but saw no reason to put anyone in the way who didn't need to be there. If the Yanks had decided to call open season on Alder, the least I could do was be grateful.

'Then be sure to thank your people for me. I didn't want to have to hurt you a second time.'

'You weren't really going to torture me though, right? You Brits don't do that sort of thing.'

'No more than you Yanks knock over the occasional inconvenient government.'

'Oh.' He looked a little surprised by that. 'And they say you guys are pussies. Glad to see it ain't true.' I got up from the couch and he offered his hand. 'Well, good hunting.'

'Thanks.' I shook hands with him, feeling the gel he'd smeared them with in an attempt to get my fingerprints. That raised a smile from me that he took for friendliness, and I was happy to give him the illusion. He'd be grinning all night until he discovered that I was wearing the Dalai Lama's fingerprints on a thin coating of plastic over my own. I couldn't help laughing on my way back to the car thinking about him trying to imagine a group of elite

Buddhist monks fighting evil – all orange robes and flying kicks. Silly idea, really, since they're much more subtle than that when you meet them in real life; and they tend to prefer J. Edgar Hoover's dabs when they're wearing falsies.

The next morning I sat down in the unit with the three discs I'd obtained from Miss Marsh. If Annie was to be believed then we were seven days from the hit, and I figured that if we could take out the gun end of the job conventionally then my end could be wrapped up in its own sweet time. I knew that we had to get the information in Annie's head off the street before it started spreading; but she couldn't hide for ever and the moment she broke the surface I'd be there. The redhead had indeed started singing as soon as she discovered that her friends wanted her dead, on the condition that she was given protection and a new identity, and the first disc had her file, her statement and the first couple of hours of video with transcripts. That last went straight to hard copy and I sat down to see what this pretty little cop-killer had to say for herself.

She'd been independent since surviving the arrest of her previous cell a few years previously, making a living mostly as a consultant to small, new groups with lots of enthusiasm and very little ability. Then she'd been contacted by a man whose name and work she knew, who suggested a meeting. That meeting had turned into a team of fifteen, all highly motivated and with the skills and equipment necessary to take the job on. She'd not been made aware of the target during the initial phase of training, and had only discovered her role in the set-up when she'd been briefed on her target: DS Fuller. Her job was to get close to him and find out what she could, but he'd been a good boy and never discussed work. This had been circumvented with the help of a little vial of clear liquid that she used to spike Fuller's drink before bedtime. The vial had been supplied just before she met him each evening, so presumably freshness was an issue in order for them to take such a risk. With that inside him, and supplied with a list of questions, she'd been able to empty the poor bloke of everything he knew. Finally, when she'd got what she needed and more besides that would come in handy as an extra income source, she'd stopped fighting the urge to do away with him. She went on a bit about this, how much she'd disliked being with an enemy of the people, and her sacred duty to free everyone from their bonds and all that, so I hit fast forward until the transcript got interesting again. She knew there was another group involved, but no more about it than that. The liaison from that group was a woman, and she brought the truth drug to the attack group at their weekly meetings. It was a shame she didn't know what happened in those meetings, but I was pretty sure that it was one of the Sisters giving orders and the gunmen obeying them.

There was more, but it related to her earlier work with other groups: a subject that didn't interest me at all. She'd come from a decent enough middle-class background, caught politics at university, then became a radical and decided that she'd found the way to solve all humanity's ills if we'd just be reasonable and listen to her. That path ended up with her planting her first bomb at the age of

twenty-two, and in the seven years since then she'd gone
through eight bombs, over a dozen murders, two kid-
nappings and the lives of sixty-seven people – all in the
name of peace, universal brotherhood and understanding.
Apparently, persuading people to listen to her message
had been more of a challenge than she had originally
expected, and it was starting to make her doubt if it was
really worth all the effort. There was a definite sense that
she was glad at the chance of a new life, grateful that
someone had stopped her. Maybe she was: I knew I would
be if someone offered me a second chance.

Her boyfriend was claiming to be a civilian who
thought that his girl was a sales rep. It was such a ridiculous
story that it might even have been true, but there was the
small matter of an assault rifle under the bed to be discussed, along with the fake passports for both of them,
the package holiday to North Africa he'd booked in the
false names and a substantial stack of several currencies
under the floorboards. I'd leave MI5 to figure that one
out, but was grateful that they'd chosen to make a run for
it rather than risk the noise of gunfire first. The Hippies
might be a talented bunch of healers, but even they'd have
trouble if I was dead.

The third and final subject was the one I'd interrupted,
a man with a body count higher than mine. He started
with the usual guff about lawyers and moved on to unlaw-
ful arrest, detention without charge and the rest of the
civil rights crap that makes me glad I can ignore it. If I
had to worry about due process of law I'd never get
anything done, but since he'd officially been picked up
by a policeman investigating something else who then

discovered our friend was wanted for questioning, the poor sod didn't have a chance. It was suggested that he was in fact lucky to have been rescued from such a perilous situation. After all, what kind of dangerous maniac kidnaps people as they go about their lawful business, and what horrors would that lead to? Things far worse than the legal system could inflict upon him, that was certain. Despite the great fortune that had led him to the interrogation room, he remained unwilling to show his gratitude by answering any questions, and wouldn't even confirm any of the names he'd used over the years.

Some people just have no sense of civic duty. It breaks the heart, really it does.

What was important to me was that the one canary of the group had basically confirmed that they were involved with the Sisterhood, which meant that finding their colleagues would allow me to stop the hit dead in its tracks. Even assuming the Sisterhood were set on killing the PM, they would have to find a whole new bunch of people to pull the trigger and that would take time. It would also require them to come out of hiding to find the right people and that would be my fallback position if I needed one.

I hit the lunchtime news and discovered that the plot had been announced. The PM was unsurprisingly refusing to change his schedule, claiming that he wouldn't be swayed by naughty people with guns and that he had complete faith in the good people with guns who looked after him. Bloody great. One of the many things I hate about politicians (and there's a long list) is the grandstanding, their habit of talking big while everyone else does all the work. Not just me, either, but the ones who can be credited for their efforts and only get recognition when somebody needs a distraction – medal or humiliation, it doesn't matter to the politicians as long as they keep their slimy noses clean. This particular example of the spin doctor's black art meant that Special Branch and MI5 would now have to hunt a bunch of people who knew they were blown rather than just wondering what had happened to the guy tasked to kill Fuller's killer. I wished them the very best of luck.

The unit had a secure telephone line and scrambler fitted, and when the handset started flashing I automatically knew it was going to be the Boss. It wasn't like him to be breathing down my neck so hard, and I guessed that there was pressure coming from further up the food chain to get things taken care of sooner rather than later. I picked up the phone and announced its identification number. The Boss announced his, and then it was time for a friendly chat.

'Was it you that gave MI5 their latest toys?'

'Yes, sir, it was. I thought it was worth the minor risk involved.'

'Minor risk? You handed over primary witnesses in your own case to another service for interrogation. That alone restricts the information we can get since Five don't have all the options we do. What were you thinking?'

'That it was the perfect weapon to neutralise Miss Marsh's interest, sir. She's taken the credit for bringing them in, so admitting the truth would be embarrassing. She's also supplied copies of secret files and recordings to someone she can't positively identify, which means prison for her if she's exposed. I've got her two ways, and if gratitude ever runs out then I've got threats to back it up.'

'Hmm.' The Boss sounded as if he didn't want to admit that I'd pulled something useful there, so I let him continue. 'What were you doing in her flat?'

'Sending her a message, sir. Letting her know that I knew far more than she did.'

'We know where you live?'

'Just so. Locating her at lunch was a reinforcement of that, so hopefully she'll find better things to do with her career. She's trying to get into fieldwork anyway, which might cut down on her free time a bit. Can anything be done to help that along, sir?'

'Possibly, yes. I like the logic, too: she might just get herself killed in the field, which would solve the problem nicely. I'll see what can be done.'

'Thank you, sir.' I didn't actually *want* to get the woman killed, just shut her up: she was good at her job and on our side in the bigger picture. I don't have a problem with eliminating the bad guys, but there wasn't any mileage in removing her from the picture permanently.

'What else is happening?'

The Boss's sharp tone brought me back to things I could do something about. 'I'm reviewing the information to see if it can give me anything new. The Sisterhood are down to seven including Annie, and if my theory is correct, then that makes them still potentially able to run their end of things. If Five can get one of their guests, presumably the assassin, to crack the location of the trigger group's base then we'll be able to render the plan non-operational and save the PM's skin – which at least solves the immediate problem.'

'Doesn't do much about the leak, though, does it? I want her back, and alive if you can. The least we can do is try to return her to her regular self.'

I had a strong suspicion that this last bit was for my benefit: nobody likes to think they'll just be taken out if something goes wrong, but the Boss had forgotten that I was somewhat clearer about things than that. If we got Annie back, the best she could hope for would be retirement, and that was likely to be somewhere quiet with quilted rubber wallpaper.

'I'll do what I can, sir, but my prime concern lies with Hamilton and Alder. The rest can be mopped up quietly if we find a way to take the head off the beast. If they get clear then there's nothing to stop them regrouping to try something else in the future.'

'Then you'd better get on with it, hadn't you? Keep me informed.'

'Yes, sir.' Then a click, and he was gone.

Someone was definitely applying pressure to him, or something else was going on. Then an idea hit me: what if the only people Annie could identify were me, the Boss and his assistant Piers? Would that mean the Boss was facing the same damage control measures that I was? I had to admit it was an entertaining way to introduce democracy into the Service and give him an idea of what it was like to be on the front line, but the idea of ending up buried next to him was not what made me smile. We didn't like each other, so the odds of getting a decent conversation going were a bit slim. Maybe we'd end up in

Kensal Green, and then Geoff and I could split our time between the amorous Goth kids and giving the old man some stick.

Having thought about it for a second or two I decided I wasn't quite ready to get killed. Maybe it would be better to find out where the Sisterhood were hiding, take care of them and then have a nice holiday somewhere perfectly mundane, ideally somewhere with a well-stocked bar.

I needed to interrogate one of the trigger group myself, and not in any of the nice, modern, non-invasive ways we normally used. There was a little something I could try if I had a quiet five minutes with one of them, and it was available on request if the circumstances warranted it. In this case, I thought they did.

All I needed was a location, and it was another six hours before my phone rang again. This time it was Piers.

'Five just broke the third man, and he's given up their base.'

'Can we substitute our own team for theirs?'

'Does this have anything to do with your requisition?'

'Yes. I won't be able to do anything once they're in and accounted for.'

'Then get over to Hereford and await orders.'

'I'm on my way.'

More high-speed driving, this time heading for a small camp that supposedly belongs to the Army, not too far from where the SAS hang their hats when they aren't off saving the material world. The road was empty for the most part, and I made good time. As I cleared the second set of gates and moved into the camp proper, a figure stepped out and waved me to a stop.

'They're waiting for you in building seven. I'll show you.' The figure, an anonymous bloke in his late twenties, got into the car and directed me to the staging area. I didn't know his face, but he appeared to know mine – he was probably one of the guys who pulled me out of Pickerell House – and started rattling off instructions as we drove.

'You'll be "Cutter" again for this run. We go in first, then you follow up when we say. Keep your head down and stay out of our lines of fire. If we tell you to drop, then you don't get up until you're told. Understood?'

'I'm not exactly a pen-pusher, mate.'

'I didn't say you were, but we're used to working as a team. A lone wolf in the middle of that can screw things up and get people killed, so while you ride with us you play by our rules; and our rules say if you're not a member of the team then you're a passenger. Passengers work to the same set of rules no matter who they are, and if you can't work with that then you're welcome to stay here.'

'Then I suppose I'll follow the rules.'

'Don't suppose anything, just do as you're told,' he said as we pulled up and got out of the car. Inside building seven was a group of men in assault gear, checking each other over and making their weapons ready for transport. I was pointed towards a pile of kit similar to theirs and changed into it as the final briefing got under way.

Chapter Nineteen

We rocketed through the night in four souped-up 4x4s. My hosts hadn't even bothered telling me where we were going beyond 'the Target', and weren't hugely conversational as we travelled. There were last-minute radio checks, weapons were loaded, straps tightened and then an air of quiet, professional tension settled over the occupants of my vehicle. This wasn't my first time riding with a strike team, although the guy who'd been assigned to look after me behaved as though it was. He did have a point: I prefer to work alone, and I'm used to it. These guys were different, each a cog in a finely tuned machine that did a job similar to mine, but with far more chance of things going wrong. Friendly fire, for example, wasn't really something I worried about in the middle of a hit but it was a major hazard for them if people didn't do their jobs exactly the way they should. They drilled while I improvised, and having me improvise in the middle of their drill held a very real danger of getting someone killed who wasn't on the list of hostiles. So I kept my neck wound in, did as I was told and let them worry about securing the area for me.

I sometimes wonder where the Service gets these people from. The strike teams don't have the kind of esoteric skills I use, focusing mainly on the techniques used to introduce others to the mysteries that exist after death as quickly and efficiently as possible, so I suppose they could come from anywhere. I've noticed that they tend to be pretty blasé about the odder parts of their equipment, though, so I imagine they must get some kind of introduction to the subject before they're allowed out in the field. Only they know for sure, and they weren't overly interested in long personal conversations about where we'd all come from; not that I was likely to tell them the truth about me, either.

I was given the five-minute warning signal, and checked my own weapons for the last time. The strike team were carrying silenced SMGs as their primary armament, with pistols for back-up. I didn't rate a machine gun, but was much happier using my knife with a silenced pistol in reserve. My main tool for this job was sitting in a large pouch in my webbing, and if everything went according to plan it would be the closest thing to a weapon I'd have to use.

The vehicles pulled in and we got out and assembled in silence. The leader signalled to his men via hand gestures, and two by two they disappeared into the night until only my handler and I remained. We were to wait until the all-clear came through.

The minutes crawled by as everyone found their appointed positions, then finally the radio came quietly to life as each team counted off ready. The order was given to start the attack.

More waiting interspersed with status reports. It was frustrating as hell listening to other people fighting my battle for me. The only thing that kept me in place was the knowledge that the only effect my presence would have down there would be to screw things up. Didn't mean I had to like it, though. At long last the call I'd been waiting for: 'Area secured. Cleared for passenger.' My handler led me around the side of a hill and the target came into sight. It was a small farmhouse with lights on in the windows, and a couple of outbuildings in darkness. Shadowy figures moved between them, having made sure they were free of unwelcome surprises, and when they looked at us my handler gave them the recognition signal.

Once we were indoors, I removed my gas mask and gloves. I needed to see the people I was dealing with clearly, and I wanted to get everything right. I'd only worked with this kit once before, but it had taught me to be very careful about what I did and I fully intended to apply those lessons this time. Against one wall was a pile of eight dead bodies in hand- and ankle cuffs, a safety precaution I approved of. While I wasn't expecting any of them to get up and start fighting again, it was nice to know they'd have trouble doing it. Opposite them was a row of five people kneeling with their faces to the wall, also cuffed at wrists and ankles and guarded by a man at each end. Judging by the state of their clothes, my guess was that the living had been asleep when the team hit, and the dead guys on guard. I looked at one of the guys who was watching the survivors.

'Is this all of them?' My reply came as a nod. 'Right, then.' I turned my attention to the prisoners. 'OK, you lot, listen up. I have one question for you: who was responsible for liaising with the other group? Answer quickly and everything will go as well as it can. Fuck me about and it gets nasty.'

'Fuck you, pig.' My respondent was right in the middle of the prisoners, the rest of whom sniggered in support of his rapier wit. I kicked him in the small of the back, just between where his wrists were pinned.

'Within two hours I will know everything I need to, and more, so this is your second chance. Who was the liaison?'

Silence.

'Last chance to answer. After this we get unfriendly.'

Not a single word.

'Oh well, don't say I didn't try.' I opened the pouch with my special toy in it and pulled out a tightly wrapped bundle, which I unrolled on the table that sat against one wall. Inside was a spike made of gold-like metal and covered in hieroglyphs. According to the file on this thing, it had been picked up by an ex-RAF officer while he was in Egypt, and was perfect for moments like this. I considered my options, sizing up who was going to be my first subject. There really was only one choice: the gobby one in the middle. At my signal, he was grabbed by each arm and dragged backwards into the next room. I followed the group, the spike in my right hand as I hefted it to find the balance point and get used to the weight. Gobby looked at me, realising that since I was showing my face he might actually be in trouble. Obviously he knew the first rule of taking prisoners: if you're going to release them alive, never let them see a face they can describe to anyone else.

I signalled for the others to leave us alone, then stood

in front of my prisoner just out of his reach. He may have been bound hand and foot but I wasn't going to give him a chance to use his head. I looked him up and down, noticing nothing of particular interest; he was just another scumbag who stood between me and my objective. I used to have feelings about people like this, but when I looked at it objectively I came to the conclusion that they were willing participants in the game. After all, if the man in front of me hadn't chosen to be rude he may well have been back next door while someone else was in here with me, and he was in this place as a result of the choice he had made to be a bad guy. He would have done the same to me if our roles had been reversed.

Eventually I spoke. 'Last chance. Tell me who the liaison with the other group was. I shan't ask nicely again, but you will tell me – one way or the other.'

This one really had some balls. He looked up at me, then spat at my face as best he could. I was impressed. His last action in this life was one of defiance, and I only hope I've got the courage to go out that way when my time comes around. Of course, he didn't know that he was about to die there and then; he thought I was going to torture him for a bit then try a few more questions before I finally got round to it. I could see him preparing to be hit again, marshalling his strength and forcing himself to breathe slowly and easily to help him keep his head. Splendid preparation, exactly the sort of thing I'd do under the same circumstances.

It was also a complete waste of time.

He watched as I poured charcoal powder into a bowl, then put a flame to it. Once it was smouldering nicely, I added incense from a cloth bag and let it waft around the room. He'd been expecting me to hit him, so this was already putting him outside his comfort zone. As the heavy smell settled around us, I performed a couple of breathing exercises to settle myself down. I knew what was coming, and wanted to be ready for it. It took a couple of minutes for all this to happen, and by the time we were good to go he was starting to sweat. I picked up the spike, walked up to stand in front of him, looked him straight in the eye and brought the spike down right through the top of his skull.

The room lurched. His eyes went wide as pain exploded inside him and he started to die. The spike had penetrated deep into his brain, through the cerebrum and down into the hippocampus. Somewhere in the distance I could hear screaming, then the ride began.

I'm at school somewhere in Eastern Europe, being teased because I'm the wrong religion. Someone is punching me, and I go down bleeding and angry.

A different school, now one of the tormentors. Kicking another kid who is down on the floor. Blood spills from his mouth, and the sight of it makes me feel good.

In the middle of a gunfight, wearing the uniform of a soldier. There are women and children running around, trying to get away. They don't worry me yet – someone else is responsible for rounding them up, and we'll deal with them once we've taken the village.

Drinking with a group of intense young men, arguing about how the world could be made a better place.

A softly spoken man telling me there is a way I can help

with the struggle for my people's freedom. Meeting more of them, feeling as if I belong here.

Setting my first bomb, feeling the pride of a job well done when I see it explode in the middle of the street, feeling the lack of emotion that comes from knowing the dead people don't matter.

Standing round a table in a building somewhere hot and sandy, while a man shows me how to place bombs in a petrol refinery.

Teaching a group of young men how to shoot their Kalashnikov rifles.

Being recruited for a new job, a special team. Flying to England on a false passport.

The team meeting for the first time. I recognise some of the names: they have done great things for the cause.

The plan being explained. How we will strike at the enemy's heart and destabilise their government. One of the other group is here: a woman who seems to have inside knowledge. I do not like her, nor do I trust her. Something about her is wrong.

Another meeting, with one member of the group explaining that there may be some danger of the authorities discovering our plan. Making new plans to escape if things go wrong.

The liaison explaining that the other group has been compromised, but that the operation is still to go ahead. There will be one more meeting before the attack, then no more contact before the night we execute the plan. More talk, then kissing one of the women goodnight as she goes to guard duty and I go to bed. Some noises in the darkness, then a man in black pointing a gun at me. Being dragged into the kitchen, seeing my lover halfway down a pile of dead bodies as I am forced to face the wall. Questions from behind me, which I answer with the contempt they deserve, then I am grabbed and dragged backwards by two of the men in black. I see a third man, a man whose face is uncovered, and know that I am going to die. I start to pray quietly inside my head and prepare myself for the torture that is to come. Everyone knows that these people torture and murder no matter how much they deny it. The man looks at me as if I am nothing more than an animal. He asks his question again, but I am strong. I shall resist him. Now he acts strangely, with incense and a metal rod. He stands above me, staring into my eyes, then he raises his hand . . .

I let go of the spike just as it was coming down and fell back onto the carpet, my head spinning. There was a wastebasket near me, and I got to it just in time as what felt like the last week's worth of food shot out of me in heave after heave.

After a few minutes I was able to stand again. The dead man's memories filtered down through my own, changing into a collection of stories as my own personality reasserted itself. There was nothing left of him now bar the empty shell on the carpet, no life beyond, no redemption, no paradise. The spike had eaten his soul and given me the information in his memories as they flashed before his eyes on the way out. It was quite a ride.

I rinsed my mouth with water, removed the spike from what I now knew to be Vaclav's head and threw his body into a corner, then went back out into the kitchen. Alexei –

the liaison – was on the far left of the line, and I signalled for him to be brought in for a chat.

When he saw Vaclav in the corner, Alexei started to struggle and got a smack on the back of the head for his efforts. The two faceless men who brought him in left as quickly as they could, leaving us alone together.

'Alexei, I want you to listen to me for a moment. You won't leave this room alive, and all you can do is make your peace with whichever god you follow. You made the mistake of getting in with some very bad people, and this is the price you must pay for it. It's nothing personal, but I don't have the time to beat information out of you and I know you won't give it to me willingly. It's just business, Alexei, just business.' By now the incense smoke had filled the room, working its way into our lungs and from there to the bloodstream. He swayed a little as he looked up at me.

'I do not fear you. You will lose eventually, and you will die. Perhaps not by my hand, but by one like mine. You were damned before you were born, and the instrument of that damnation travels towards you even now. There will be great celebration when it happens, for whenever one of your number—'

I was bored of this and regretting having said anything at all, so I shut him up with the spike.

His family had money when he was a child, and lost it when things went wrong in his part of the world. He used his convictions to hide a desire for revenge against those who wronged him, the countries who stood back and allowed the chaos to take his family, their money and their land. There was a similar trail to Vaclav's into terrorism, and they'd known each other for a while: Vaclav had recommended him for this job, apparently.

Finally we got to the good bits involving his contact with the Sisterhood. They'd done a bit of a number on him. He was plied with drugged drinks and a couple of the women entertained him in some very imaginative ways. He experienced pleasure that few sane people will ever understand, and Alder used it cleverly. His love for her grew along with loyalty to the Sisterhood. He might have been a member of the 11/11 trigger group but he belonged to Alder, heart, mind, body and soul. He grew to look forward to the meetings, to the chance to be near her. He needed to serve her, lived to make her happy. The operation had to succeed because she willed it and he finally understood that he lived only to be an instrument of that will. Her face was never far from his thoughts, and in his dreams he was her loyal slave for the rest of time.

There were more orders, plans for the hit and afterwards. Protocols to make sure that the rest of the group knew nothing about the Sisterhood that would aid the authorities. Hamilton had met with the whole group once but had been disguised, and all contact now came through Alexei. He was very proud of this in his heart, but careful not to let the others know of the glorious rewards he received for his service. He pretended to his friends that he didn't like the job, fearing that if they knew the truth he would never be allowed to see his mistress again, never know the touch of her hand on his neck as he sank to his knees before her.

There was a lot more, but you get the idea. By the time we got to the end, his terror when he heard the screams from next door, being dragged in to face me and his speech, I was sick of the whole thing. It turned out that he was about to tell me that his mistress would come for me, because he truly believed that. He had no god now but Candace Alder.

He was better off dead.

Once I'd lost another week of food I cleaned up my gear. The still-burning incense went into the fireplace and the hot bowl into a heatproof container. The spike was almost as hot as the bowl, and it surprised me that I hadn't burned my hand on the thing. I found Alexei's room and helped myself to a few things, then, nursing a headache from when he'd been pistol-whipped earlier, I returned to the main group.

'Thanks, gentlemen, that's all I need.' The strike team looked at our remaining three prisoners.

'What about them?' asked one faceless trooper.

'They had a huge argument that ended in a gunfight among themselves. It's a horrible thing when fanatics lose it.'

'Right. You'd better head back.' I took the hint and left the farmhouse, barely hearing the three silenced shots that began the process of covering our activities. By the time we pulled away from the pick-up point, a dull red glow from the burning farmhouse filled the horizon.

Chapter Twenty

It had taken long enough, but finally I had the break I'd been looking for. As long as we kept the trigger group's unfortunate demise a secret, there was one more meeting planned before the night of the hit and thanks to Alexei I knew exactly where and when it was to be held. All I had to do was show up and look enough like the guy to get Candace in close. It was a perfect plan; the meeting was in a public place that could be loaded with back-up and then all we'd have to do was stage a police raid to come in and make the whole thing look legit.

It even gave me a day off, since I had to wait for Saturday night. Having spent all of Thursday and much of Friday morning sleeping off the raid and the spike's effects, most of it went on meditation to finish straightening me back out, and the rest was devoted to studying defences against glamours – the forms of magic used to screw with people's heads. It would have been a bit embarrassing if I got my hands on the woman and she made me let her go, or sent me in the wrong direction entirely.

The following afternoon was spent with a make-up box. Since I couldn't rely on magic to disguise me, it needed to be done the old-fashioned way, with wig, contact lenses and subtle changes to my skin tone. Alexei and I were about the same size and build, so his clothes were a good fit and had the advantage of having his aura on them to help my illusion. The meet was scheduled for midnight, and we were ready in plenty of time. The strike team went in slowly, in small numbers, positioning themselves to cover the building and provide support wherever it was needed. Then it was time for me to make my entrance.

Club Yoni was an underground fetish event that moved about from month to month. It counted MPs, judges and a couple of senior police officers as members and had a strict policy that everyone wore a mask at all times to preserve anonymity. That way, it was a safe place for everyone to let go and indulge whatever desires they needed to let loose. Other items of clothing were purely optional. Like every other club of its type, I found this one pretty dull. I get as interested in the sight of a hot woman in spray-on rubber as the next guy, but the moment a fat middle-aged man in a nappy walks by the mood is as dead as a dodo for me. The main dance floor had a bar at one end, a stage at the other and darkened booths running down both sides. Both sides had a doorway, through which I could see a variety of racks and equipment that would have been right at home in a medieval dungeon, or back at Pickerell House. The place was just starting to warm up, and I could see at least a couple of people hanging up already having the shit beaten out of them by their owners.

I made my way to the bar, grabbed a cranberry juice (disgusting stuff, but Alexei seemed to like it – another advantage of using the spike over normal interrogation is getting information like that) and found a spot near one of the doorways. On the floor, people were dancing to something loud and full of bleeps, and I could make out a wide variety of people interfering with each other in some of the booths. Now all I could do was wait, and hope that my disguise was sufficiently convincing without the rubber underpants and butt plug.

Almost exactly on the stroke of midnight I felt someone moving behind me, and a pair of hands slid slowly around my head to cover my eyes. There was a whisper in my ear, clear over the music.

'Mistress says you're mine tonight.'

The speaker didn't get any further as I turned around to face Juliet Mooney with a smile. A different member of the inner circle, but a member all the same. Early thirties, blonde, skinny under her black leather catsuit, and with a pretty face covered by a mask of black ostrich feathers that helped her deep blue eyes stand out like sapphires.

'Guess again, love,' I said with a grin as she pulled her arms away and found them being grabbed from behind by a large man in a gimp mask. The handcuffs were on before she knew what was happening, and a ball gag stopped her trying anything to mess with our heads – I had no evidence to expect that from Juliet, but better safe than sorry and the plan was designed for someone we knew could. Her eyes widened as she realised just how screwed she was, then the last part of the capture plan went into action as a spray hypodermic injected a large dose of hypnotic straight into her bloodstream. She was as docile as a sleepy kitten in under a minute.

'Come on, Juliet, I've got a much nicer place for us to

play.' And with that we led her out of the club and into a waiting van. Fifty quid to the doorman and a little mind magic convinced him that it was all part of her fantasy, one she'd probably thank him for personally and at some length later.

As soon as we were in the van I was working on a spell to keep us invisible to anyone who might be watching remotely. The files didn't tell me if any of the group were psychic enough to do it on their own, but they were certainly good enough magicians to make use of a crystal ball. At least this way they'd get static, and hopefully assume that it was us trying to get at them blindly rather than anything this deliberate. A chancy plan, but worth a try.

I'd picked a deserted warehouse for this part of the operation, having decided that using one of our own sites carried too much potential risk if anything went wrong. The warehouse in question had been built over the site of a secret temple from the Renaissance, one used by a variety of weirdos right up until the Georgian era, so the ground was already primed for operation and just needed a quick blessing to remind it of what it used to be. I'd made sure that was done before we began the night's work.

My first instinct was to use the spike again, but I'd pushed my luck using it twice on the trigger group and there was a real danger that overexposure to the thing would start warping my mind, making me want to use it more and more. That had happened during the war, apparently: it had been used on a batch of German prisoners who had information that was needed in a hurry and the poor sod doing it had ended up in an asylum thanks to a combination of information overload and the spike's nature. I wasn't cleared to know if anyone else could use it, which meant I couldn't get help that way, so I had to find an alternative – and this was it.

A huge glyph was marked out on the ground, with a space in the middle where Juliet had been spread-eagled on her back, her arms and legs outstretched and tied to stakes in the ground by a couple of guys from the strike team; then we just had to wait for the drugs to work their way out of her system. That was going to take a good hour, and I used the time to remove the disguise. I hadn't enjoyed being Alexei, and was glad to get back into myself.

Then it was time to work. Candles to light, incense to burn: all the usual ritual rigmarole, and a load of chanting from my little book of Latin to get the details just right. I stepped into the circle and approached Juliet. She was looking a little dreamy, but still wasn't too pleased to see me. 'We'll get you, little man,' she said. 'You can't stop us.'

'Really? You hardly seem in a position to be that confident.'

'We'll use you as a plaything, and you'll like it when we're done with you.'

'No, Juliet, I really don't think so. I think I'm going to hunt each one of you down and kill you. Some will get it easy, if they're lucky, but you ... You're going to suffer.' I might as well have been reciting Shakespeare to her for all the effect it was having on her expression, but I kept going. 'I'm going to hurt you, Juliet. Then I'm going to hurt you again. Over and over and over until I finally let you die. But it's going to take a long time. You'll beg me to kill you, and I'll just hurt you some more. Threaten me all you like, but no one can find you here, no one can hear you, and no one – not even your beloved Sisters – can save you. You belong to me.' I could see it was starting to sink in – Juliet was trying to scream for help psychically and getting no further than the shield surrounding the circle. 'See? If they can't hear you then they can't save you. Poor little Juliet, all alone. No one to save her from the Big Bad Wolf.' She tried screaming normally for a bit, and I let her have her head. 'The building's soundproof, so no one can hear you. It's just you and me now. Just poor little Juliet and the Big Bad Wolf.' I could see tears in her eyes as panic started to grip her. The combination of helplessness and suggestions was starting to play on basic fears from childhood: being alone, getting hurt and the monsters in the dark – in this case the classic fairy-tale wolf. I wanted her scared out of her wits to the point of being incoherent, and we were heading in the right direction. I considered what to do next, whether to work her over physically or psychologically. Both had their good and bad points and I was pushing for fast results that would last long enough to achieve everything I wanted. Decision made, I produced my dear old fighting knife and held it where she could see it.

'Do you see this, Juliet? Do you want to know how many people I've killed with this knife? Quite a few, I can tell you. More than anyone will ever know, and I'll never go to prison for it. The authorities know all about it, but they'll never stop me; and when I kill you, you'll just be one more corpse that nobody cares about. Thrown away like rubbish and forgotten before you're cold.' She was really starting to lose it now, so I decided to take it up a level. Moving very slowly, I used my knife to cut her clothes off. The thin leather she'd worn to Club Yoni parted under the edge like a flower opening, and as each garment fell to the floor her breathing rate went up, her pupils dilated and already flushed skin darkened further. She started screaming again, and I slapped her face hard to shut her up, shouting abuse at her as I did so. This was different from what she'd been through with the Sisterhood in one very important aspect: while she believed that she'd submitted to Alder voluntarily, here it was forced. The power dynamic was entirely different, with no comfort zone, no safe-word to make it stop and no expectation of pleasure or reward. This was what the inner circle had done to the outer, a breaking of the will by force rather than by subtlety. By the time she was naked, I could see her eyes starting to show the ragged edge of insanity. I took a spare candle and dripped hot wax on her for a while, letting her see pleasure on my face each time she reacted, then reached for the riding crop . . .

One of the advantages to spending as much time in hospital as I do is that it gives you time to read while you wait for the stitches to heal and the bones to mend. I discovered Plato in hospital, and Descartes, and Kipling. I adore Kipling; his tales of life in India gave me a real hunger to learn more about that time, and eventually I discovered tiger hunting. One of the tricks tiger hunters used to employ was known as a 'Judas goat': a goat would be tied to a stake in a clearing, and the hunters would position themselves with a clear shot to it. The goat's cries would attract the tiger, the tiger would attack the goat and the sahib soon had a new rug for his drawing room. Juliet was my Judas goat.

Now, as much as I hate the idea of sounding like a whiny little bitch, I really wasn't enjoying this. Torturing people isn't exactly my idea of a good time, but as I told Annie back in Bristol it's the less shitty alternative to lynch mobs and anarchy. I choose my targets carefully – having spent the time necessary to identify the right place to apply pressure where a mob would just cut loose and burn your house down with everyone in it. While 'It's not as wrong as the other options' isn't much of an excuse, I'm not a serial killer or a psycho: I'm a surgeon. Just as I'd had to pretend with Benny, I had to give Juliet the idea that I was enjoying it so she'd have more reason to fear me. If I was dealing with a pro I'd let him see me as bored but just doing my job, but since she was a zealot she needed to see that same passion in me, to allow her to understand just how far this could go.

This is how your freedoms are defended, and one of those freedoms is ignorance of its price.

Now that I had Juliet up to fever pitch, it was time to put part two of the plan into action. I dropped the shield for ten seconds, allowing her psychic cry for help to escape, then threw it back up. Enough for the Sisterhood to realise that she was in a great deal of trouble, but that she'd managed to get a shout out before we'd stopped her. Enough for Juliet to realise that she'd been able to get a message out, to give her a little hope that I could take away again.

I could see that hope in her eyes, driving the panic down. It was just enough to give her something to hang on to, a prayer that she might be rescued when her sisters came to save her.

'They're coming,' she said. 'They're coming to get you now.'

'I hope so, Juliet. That's why I let them hear you. The building's surrounded with armed men, and when they come they'll be shot to pieces. You've just killed them all.'

'No.' A whisper, wanting to disbelieve but seeing no real reason to doubt me.

'Oh yes.' I smiled. I could feel something trying to penetrate the shield from outside, an attempt by the Sisterhood to re-establish contact. That was exactly what I wanted, since all I then had to do was get a trace on that to find out where they were hiding. I had maps to hand, and a little silver necklace that I'd taken from Juliet to use as a dowsing pendulum. The necklace was pretty: a flower made with Celtic knotwork from a pentagram, which I'd seen a couple of times on books at Pickerell House, and around Annie's neck and those of the two women I'd already taken out. I guessed that it was the closest thing they had to a badge, and it seemed perfect for what I had in mind now. It was barely a couple of minutes' work to find that they were back in Bristol, hiding in one of the poorer parts of town on an estate with a rough reputation. That suited me: the locals wouldn't even be overly surprised to see a police raid going on. I established a shield over the centre of the circle where Juliet was, stepped outside of the main barrier and sealed it again behind me. Two layers now separated Juliet from the Sisterhood, the psychic equivalent of double glazing, and that would hold for much longer than I needed.

'Well done, Juliet, and thanks for your help,' I said, and she screamed obscenities at me as I got into my car and drove away. I think she'd have been less pissed off if I'd actually needed to hit her, rather than having played her so easily.

The strike team weren't far behind me, since I'd want them in their police uniforms to help me in Bristol. However, while I'd been dealing with Juliet, some of them had been busy as well. The whole warehouse had been wired with explosives, and if anyone set foot inside the place it was rigged to collapse in on itself with a fairly impressive bang that could be blamed on a faulty gas main. That way, if the Sisterhood did somehow manage to get a track on Juliet, my promise would come true and everyone would be killed quickly and efficiently. It also had the advantage of not giving Alder any human ears upon which she could employ her particular skills. Orders to shoot on sight are all very well, but there's always an 'X' factor that you can't predict. Despite her formidable reputation, I doubted even Candace Alder could sweet-talk twenty kilos of C-4.

I needed to square up what was going to happen next, and that meant calling the Boss. I risked using a scrambled cellphone to get him out of bed so I could explain the plan and get his approval to impersonate a police team. Showing up and waving an ID card is all very well and slips through with surprising ease, but having a dozen men in body armour waving guns around on a council estate is a different matter entirely. It needs the cooperation of a chain of people and the order to do that needs to be legitimate. In this case it would take the form of a couple of phone calls making us look like a joint operation between MI5 and the SAS to arrest a group of terrorists. Not that far from the truth, which is always the best kind of lie.

Back onto the M4, heading west at a hundred and twenty with the sunrise behind me. I felt better than I had for a while: more like the hunter I was supposed to be after too long stumbling along in the Sisterhood's wake. It was time for some payback, and you have no idea how much I was looking forward to that.

Chapter Twenty-One

'Gentlemen, we'd like to take as many of these women alive as we can, with one exception. Candace Alder, also known as Caroline Blake, is to be shot dead on sight. Do not let her talk to you or make eye contact – no warnings, just kill her. Believe me, it's for your own good.' I was talking to the strike team by radio as we approached Bristol. I didn't want to waste time once we got to the location, so this was the compromise. 'As far as we know it's a standard second-floor two-bedroom council flat: one door in with windows front and back. I want two people under those windows on each side, and the rest of you with me. Nobody gets out of there without our permission. Now, we're pretending to be cops, so remember your manners if you're dealing with the public. That shouldn't have to happen because the locals are going to provide us with a couple of guys to handle the public and run the outside perimeter, and I'm expecting us to be out before the media show up. It's likely that the targets know we're coming, so expect resistance. Warn if you can, but don't do anything silly. That's my piece – are there any questions?'

I clarified a couple of points as we shot through the outskirts of town and then it was five minutes to go. The local police were waiting nearby and tagged onto the end

of our convoy as we swept up in front of the block and
bailed out. Up the stairs at a run, then I was banging on
the door.

'Armed police – open up!'

I was completely unsurprised by the lack of response,
and nodded to the guy with the Enforcer. As I slid my gas
mask into position, matching my appearance to the rest
of the team, the heavy metal pipe smashed against the
hinges of the door. Splinters flew everywhere but the
entrance was still blocked: a reinforced door. Again, not a
shock that they'd fortified the place a bit. The Enforcer
went to one side and the entry man started running
detcord around the frame. Thirty seconds later there was
a loud bang and the door was lying on the hallway floor.
The first two pairs went in, covering each other as they
moved cautiously forward. At each door they reached
there was a moment as it was kicked open to bump against
the wall behind it, then movement followed by a shout of
'Clear!'

Another team went in behind them, double-checking
and ready to provide fire support as needed. That left two
guys guarding the front door along with me and my
babysitter, the same guy as last time. His opinion of me
didn't seem to have improved but I couldn't have cared
less. At least he didn't appear to have a problem with me
being in charge of this particular job, but I was glad when
the radio gave me something to do.

'Cutter, we have two targets cornered. You are cleared
to enter.'

I walked in, and felt the atmosphere change immediately. Hostile, defensive and unpleasant, with a side of

desperation. There was wreckage from the strike team's progress left and right as I moved down the corridor to the back bedroom, where two of the team moved aside to let me enter.

Inside was another fire team pointing their machine guns at two frightened but defiant-looking women armed with knives. The first was Sharon Cope, a forty-year-old accountant who was known to be the most aggressive member of the group – if not the brightest. The other one was Annie.

I swallowed. My orders were to bring Annie home to see what could be done to straighten her head out, but right now she didn't look overly keen on going anywhere.

'Annie, I need you to put the knife down.' She looked at me blankly, and I remembered the respirator. Very slowly, I reached up and pulled it back over my head to reveal my face.

'Bill?' That was good, she remembered me without immediately wanting to find a home for the knife. 'But you're ... I thought I ...'

'Not quite. Now put the knife down and we can talk about getting you out of here.'

'I ... I don't think so, Bill. You're just going to shoot us.'

'If that was the plan you'd already be dead. All I want to do is take you home so we can sort everything out. We'll go somewhere quiet and you can have a rest for as long as you need.'

'What the fuck,' asked the other woman, 'is your boyfriend doing here? I thought he was some kind of office drone.'

Annie looked confused for a second, as though two halves of her were arguing inside her head. 'He is, but ...' She shook her head as though trying to loosen something. 'No, he's a policeman. He's a consultant. I don't ...' She staggered slightly, leaning against the wall for support. Her old personality was trying to reassert itself over Alder's brainwashing. They'd worked Annie over, but not the agent underneath that cover. For a second I wished I knew her real name so I could help pull that side of her forward, but there was no time for wishing.

'Annie, put the knife down and walk to me. We're going to sort everything out, I promise.'

'You're with him, aren't you?' I was amazed it had taken Sharon this long to get the idea. 'You're a fucking *pig*?'

'Yeah, nice one, Nimrod, thanks for joining us. You can drop your knife too while we're at it, we've got questions for you.' But Sharon had no time for me, she was focused on the realisation that the Sisterhood had been betrayed from within. It's not a nice thing to have to face.

'You sold us out! You bitch!' And with that, Sharon launched herself straight at Annie, knife first. There were two bursts of fire and Sharon's chest exploded as six nine-millimetre rounds went exactly where they were supposed to: a two-inch circle just above the solar plexus. She fell onto Annie, then her momentum gave up and both women fell to the floor. Annie wore a shocked expression, eyes wide and face suddenly very pale.

I rushed forward and rolled Sharon's body away, revealing the knife handle that was buried in Annie's stomach. The handle was pointing down, which meant the blade had gone into her lungs. There was pink foam already forming on her lips and her breathing wasn't sounding so good.

'Oh shit.' It wasn't until after I recognised my own voice that I realised I'd said anything. The team medic was suddenly there, ripping Annie's clothes open to reveal the full extent of the wound. Blood was leaking out around the blade, bright red and freshly filled with oxygen. I took her hand, already cold, and held on tight.

'You're going to be OK, Annie, the doc's already working on it.' We all knew it was bullshit, but there's not much else you can say at a time like that. Blood was soaking into my clothes, warming them as Annie got colder. She coughed, a fine pink spray coming from her mouth as she did. There was more foam on her lips and each heartbeat spread more blood from the hole in her chest.

'Bill, my PDA. Directions. Password is . . .' Another cough, more of a choke as blood seeped into her windpipe. It was a toss-up whether she'd bleed out first or drown in the stuff. 'Password is inkwell. I lost it Bill, I—'

'We'll get them, Annie. Don't worry, we'll get them.'

But she wasn't listening any more.

The strike team wanted to get out as quickly as possible, so I sent them in search of Annie's bag with her PDA in it, and to find any other notebooks that might have been about the place – especially in Sharon's gear. After ten minutes they'd turned the place over, found what I wanted and bagged it up for examination. My babysitter came to find me finally putting Annie's head on the floor and replacing my mask.

'Time to go, sir,' he said.

'She was one of ours.'

'Oh.' There wasn't much else he could have said, really. 'We're moving out now. Are you ready?'

'Do I have a choice?' We got everyone back into vehicles and pulled out of the block's car park just as the first TV van arrived for the local police to deal with, and I headed back to the industrial unit to see what Annie had left us and wash the blood off.

It was strange going through Annie's belongings. Because I tend to work alone I have the luxury of not losing people very often. Not real people, anyway: informants don't count, and nor do cat's-paws. When I do work with others it's most often with a back-up guy – someone doing the job I was supposed to do for Annie. They've always been better at it than I was. When you're on the inside, the support officer is your link to the real world, a reminder that the life you're living isn't your own and the beliefs you spout aren't really yours, either. Annie had been stuck in a position where Alder reprogrammed her cover personality and the field officer underneath had been hidden under all the shit laid down during that process. She'd started to remember at the end, which meant we might have had more of a chance at getting her back than I'd thought.

What it came down to was that I'd been responsible for Annie, and I'd fucked it up. That hurt. That made it personal. Annie had fought as best she could, even managing to keep her real identity a secret – or at least it appeared so from Sharon's reaction – and I was going to make sure she had an honour guard to escort her properly into the next world.

The notebooks and Annie's PDA provided a list of possible rendezvous points that gave the remains of the Sisterhood two months to get back together. After that there were communication protocols for newspaper classified ads that could be used for years. My guess from the information was that they would try to go underground and establish new identities and then be called back when a new operation was planned, but it seemed more likely to me that they would in fact be left out to dry as a distraction. Alder and Hamilton could always make new followers pretty easily, especially with the right equipment. There were only two members of the inner circle left now apart from them and if I had to choose between a successful escape and two easily replaced stooges I knew exactly which way I'd go.

Even assuming that the rendezvous plans would be ignored by Hamilton and Alder, that still left me with a chance to deal with the other members of the inner circle. While they weren't as important as the leaders, they would still be better off the streets than on, and I didn't want to leave any loose ends. According to Annie's instructions, the first meeting was to take place the next morning in London, frighteningly close to where I'd left Juliet. A plan instantly suggested itself, and a message went straight off to the strike team, followed by a report to the Boss. He needed to know what had happened in Bristol anyway, and at least now I had good news to give him as well.

That night was spent in a warehouse less than a quarter of a mile from where Juliet lay. I'd stopped by to give her water (and check the charges) on the way, to keep her going for a little longer in case I ended up needing her again or somebody managed to pick up a faint trace and decided to investigate, and she'd been just as happy to see me as you'd expect. I took particular pleasure in telling her that two more of her sisters were dead and the rest were soon to join them.

This time I put snipers into position overlooking the access routes to the building and had a clean-up team ready to go less than a minute away. There was a snatch van as well, run by the members of the strike team who weren't on sniper duty. I wanted these women taken quickly and efficiently, without any shouting, and this was the best way to do it. We weren't expecting anyone until mid-morning, but didn't know who'd be watching or for how long. Magical shielding prevented any of the team from being spotted through scrying or remote sensing, and camouflage gear made sure they were protected from beady little eyes. I could barely make out where they were, and I knew exactly where to look.

At eleven o'clock, our patience paid off. Michaela Phillips and Sarah Madsen, the last two members of the inner circle bar Alder and Hamilton, slowly approached the building on foot. Reports came in from the snipers tracking their progress, and eventually I was able to watch for myself as they stepped into the warehouse and waited in the shadows for anyone else who made it. They were nervous, talking in whispers and trying to reassure one another that everything was going to be all right. I was getting it all through a long-range microphone, but to be honest they weren't saying anything of interest. They were just two scared women who'd finally realised exactly how out of their depth they had managed to get, and hoping that someone would give them a hand out of it. I felt sorry for them in a way: it was certain that none of this had been their intention when they joined the Sisterhood. What little pity I had wasn't going to do them any good, though; they were enemies of the nation now, to be removed in the interest of public safety and all that jazz.

An hour passed slowly, and that was the amount of time their instructions told them to wait. I started to make my way down to ground level, approaching the two women patiently. I still had a few minutes to get into position near them for the pick-up, so I made good use of it. Gentle, silent and patient, by the time they decided to go I was only about five yards away. Perfect positioning as far as I was concerned. I sent a signal to the snipers, asking if there was any activity outside with a short sequence of bleeps over the radio. The answer was negative: nothing was happening out there at all. Another signal told the snatch squad to start their engines and be ready to move, and it was confirmed immediately. As Madsen opened the door I sent the go code, and by the time the door had closed I was standing right behind it, watching through the window.

Two nondescript white vans, identical to thousands that drive the streets of London every day, screeched to a halt and I stepped out into the daylight as doors slid back to reveal armed men training their weapons on the women. One went in each vehicle and they were gone in less than ten seconds, as though nothing had happened at all. I recalled the snipers, sending them to stand off and await further orders, then stepped out into the sunlight and walked over to the warehouse Juliet was currently sharing with my car. It had been a good morning's work, and I looked forward to finding out what interrogation would pull out of our prisoners.

Juliet was where I'd left her. The fresh candles I'd put in place when I dropped off her water were burning nicely, and everything was exactly as I'd left it, which was exactly what I wanted to see. She really was a pathetic sight, lying there naked. Her hair was matted, her eyes red and puffy from crying, her wrists and ankles raw from struggling against the ropes. Now she was also effectively useless, and I had to decide what to do with her. We had two of the inner circle in custody for debriefing, and I wasn't sure that we really needed a third. Still, I had to at least try to do the right thing, and the clean-up van pulling in behind me would see to that. I stepped into the circle, pulled a hypodermic from my pocket and administered the tranquilliser. Juliet quickly slipped under, making her safe to transfer out of the area without any danger of her calling for help, and I watched as she was strapped to an ambulance trolley and loaded into the back of the van along with the candlesticks, incense burner and other paraphernalia. The charges were carefully removed from the warehouse, and soon after that the van pulled away, leaving my car and me as the only evidence that anyone had ever been there.

Something was troubling me, though. Juliet's expression as the drugs took her didn't make sense: she'd been smiling at me, as if she had a secret. That didn't make sense at all, since she knew there was no way she was going anywhere other than a secure facility run by the Service. It was the same smile she'd had when she threatened me after we'd first got to the warehouse. 'We'll get you, little man,' was what she'd said. 'We'll use you as a plaything, and you'll like it when we're done with you.'

That smile made a whole lot more sense when the pad covered my nose and mouth and all I could smell was chloroform.

Chapter Twenty-Two

I came round to find myself strapped to what felt like a cross. My arms were stretched out away from my body and my legs spread, all held in position with pretty solid-feeling restraints. My head was held in place as well: there was a band across my forehead and plates pressed against each cheek that extended forward to make a set of blinkers. Not a good way to wake up.

I fought down the wave of panic that was trying to overwhelm me, and tried to take stock of my surroundings. Not much to see, just a dark room with the wall in front of me about eight feet away. The lighting was low and indirect, but I could see lamps on the edge of my field of vision with the bulbs pointed right at me.

Then I realised that I was naked.

This whole scene was just a little bit too familiar for my liking, and the slightly swimmy feeling in my head was yet another piece of the puzzle that led me to a very uncomfortable conclusion. I started to concentrate on my breathing, working to maintain a level-headed attitude. Getting scared would lead to confusion, and that would work against my attempts to survive this. Step one: pick a point and concentrate. That worked fine until the wall started to pulse behind it, a subtle movement that seemed to match my breathing. That meant I'd been given a hallucinogenic, which would also make me imprint-vulnerable. I had to watch out for suggestions and make sure my own definition of reality was strong enough to fight off whatever was going to be implanted in my head.

'We'll use you as a plaything, and you'll like it when we're done with you.' Juliet's words coming back to haunt me. It was certainly starting to look as if I was Alder's guest, and becoming another entry on her list of victims most certainly did not appeal. I knew I could deal with the situation; all I had to do was stay in control of my own head.

Then I wondered how many others had thought the same thing at the beginning.

It felt as if hours passed before anything happened. I was getting more light-headed, and my body felt as if it was immersed in warm water. Under other circumstances it would have been pleasant, but when Candace Alder finally stepped into view any notions of comfort left my head.

She was dressed in a simple grey business suit, open at the neck and with a skirt that went all the way to the floor. Her hair was pulled back, and to be honest she reminded me of a brunette version of Penelope Marsh. My mind wandered for a second to the image of Miss Marsh in a very unprofessional position and I could feel my body reacting to the idea in an approving manner.

'Hmm, it would seem that you like my outfit,' she said, staring at my crotch. 'That's a very good start. Who knows where we could take this, mmm?' Her fingertips ran down my chest and my heart rate leapt. It felt fantastic, and reinforced the obvious effect of her suit. She skipped my crotch entirely, concentrating instead on the outside of my thighs until I moaned, a guttural sound that my conscious mind had nothing to do with. Obviously there was more than just one drug running through my system.

'If you're a good boy, I'll let you down. Not yet, of course, but when I think you've learned how to behave. I'm quite sure you know how to follow orders already, don't you?' Her fingertips were still caressing me, making it difficult to concentrate as my head swam with sensation. All I could muster as a response was more moaning.

I tried to think, look for options. As I saw it I only had two: fight her all the way to breaking point and hope that an opportunity came up, or pretend to play along and get her confident enough to let me down. Either way I needed to escape the frame – and that was something I couldn't do on my own.

'What's the point of this?' I asked, hoping to make her stop for a second so I could get my head back together. 'Why bother?'

'Because you fucked up my little game, and took away my toys. That means I need more, and I think you'll do for a start. You'll be a loyal little guard dog once I've corrected your attitude, and I think that might come in useful while I wait for my friends to arrange a ticket out of here.' She was purring in my ear, and her breath against my skin sent a shiver down my spine. I could smell her perfume: rich, dark and heavy with musk, probably loaded with pheromones as well just to add more subconscious triggers. 'You should thank me. You'll know more pleasure than you thought was possible. Serving my whims will delight you, and indulging my appetites ... Well, that's something you've got to look forward to. You'll thank me for making you my slave, I promise.' All this was giving me a hard-on that was painful, and the way my heart was racing didn't help. She looked down, then back up into my eyes. 'I think you rather like the idea, secretly. I think you want to be mine.' Her hand was caressing my waist and thighs again and my hips were straining forward, trying to hump the air, completely beyond my control. 'So aggressive, so purposeful. You'll do very well.' Then she flicked at the end of my dick with one finger, and the combination of pain and pleasure spun me out completely. By the time I was able to focus on my surroundings again she was gone.

More time passed. I tried to get some sleep, but it was impossible. My metabolism was through the roof and my erection wouldn't go away. Whatever Alder had shot me up with was obviously a potent combination, as it were. Even the feeling of air moving across my body was making me tingle. I'd lost track of everything but my nerve endings by the time Candace returned. This time she was wearing an outfit exactly like the one Juliet Mooney had worn at Club Yoni.

'I don't think this one will come off as easily as Juliet's.' Fuck, was she reading my mind? No, she'd seen me with Juliet before she jumped me. I couldn't let myself buy into her game, had to keep myself under control. If I let myself start believing in her power I wouldn't have a chance. She stroked my erection once, and my mind went blank. I'd never been so wound up, and it was pretty obvious that she knew exactly how to play my body like a piano. She knew every possible thing she could do to me, and . . . no, wait. Stop and keep it under control. Don't let her take charge.

That was bullshit. She was already in charge.

She waited for my body to stop trembling, then touched me again. The effect was even worse that time. Then she was attaching something to my scrotum.

'This will stop you from making a mess before I say you can,' she whispered, then cupped me in her hand and squeezed. It hurt like hell and I think I screamed. Tears welled up in my eyes and then suddenly she was gone again.

I must have passed out at some point, because the next thing I knew there was something wrapped around my cock. Hot, wet and moving, but I couldn't look down to see what it was. I wanted to explode, needed to relieve the pressure just for a second, but whatever Candace had put on down there was holding me back. Again that combination of pleasure and pain, the thing jerking me off versus the pressure it was causing. I blacked out again.

It was still going on when I came round, but the tension was a thousand times worse. Candace was watching me now, standing next to the frame and running her fingers over my chest. I was almost completely out of it with pleasure; the only thing keeping me from blissing out entirely was the pressure from my balls. She whispered in my ear, 'Do you want to come?'

All I could do was groan like an animal.

'I'll let you come if you ask me nicely. All you have to do is say "please".'

Again, it was just groaning from me. I couldn't have spoken if I'd wanted to.

'Just one little word and you'll feel better.'

'N-n-n-fuck you.' It was the best I could manage. Suddenly the movement downstairs quickened, and the torture was a thousand times worse. Something swept across the tip of my cock and I realised what was happening: I was getting a blow job. The best blow job in human history, judging by the way it was affecting me.

'Try again, but now it's "Please, Mistress".'

I couldn't help myself any more. I needed to let go, needed a chance to think for just a second. The words came out of nowhere, as if someone else was saying them for me.

'P-please!'

'Please what?'

'Please, Mistress!'

'There's a good boy.' She patted me on the head and smiled like an angel. 'Now you can come.' As I heard the last word, whatever device was holding me back came off and my body started shaking. I felt as if I'd died and gone to heaven. Pure pleasure overwhelmed me. I was seeing stars and my body felt as if it was about to tear itself apart. Candace watched all of this with an amused expression, like a parent watching her child do something clever. 'Feeling better now?'

I couldn't even manage a grunt. I'd been drained of energy completely as well as the obvious and if my head hadn't been strapped into place I doubt I could even have lifted it.

'Of course you are. Now say "Thank you".'

I was still having trouble remembering my name, let alone how to speak.

'Come along, now, say "Thank you, Mistress" or I won't let you do it again. Only obedient boys get rewards.'

'Tha- thank you.' She raised an eyebrow. I felt awful, as if I'd let her down. 'Thank you, Mistress,' I responded, my voice lowered like a schoolboy's.

'Well done. Let's see if you can do better next time, though, shall we?' Her fingers touched my relaxing member and suddenly it was back at attention. I could feel the pressure starting to build again. It was slow, but it was definitely there. She smiled again, and left me alone.

I wasn't happy about how I'd caved in like that, but at least my mind was clearer for a few minutes. Alder must have had assistance for that last bit, but was it Hamilton or someone else? My instincts were pointing towards the latter, since I didn't think Sadie Hamilton was likely to get down on her knees like that for me, no matter what the objective. Perhaps that was a weak spot I could exploit? I knew that I was in deep shit regardless: I had no idea where I was or how long I'd been gone, and it was almost impossible that anyone was going to come and rescue me. That meant I only had three options, and the last didn't appeal so I had to choose between escape and suicide. The idea of ending up as Candace Alder's slave was the worst, despite her promises that I'd enjoy it. In fact those promises were what scared me most of all, because I knew she was right.

Each attachment point was solid as I tried each of them in turn. No room for me to pull a hand through or tilt my head enough to see more than I was supposed to. It was a professional job, but then Candace was hardly an amateur. I had to think my way out of this soon, before I lost my mind. Either that or I had to find a way to kill myself before I stopped wanting to.

There was movement in the room again, out of view. A soft shuffling that moved around in front of me, then a touch, then those lips again. A wave of pleasure carried me off once more and I could feel something cold and slippery being rubbed around my backside. It took me a second to remember that the stuff was called lube, and my last conscious thought for a while was that I hoped it hadn't belonged to Karen Thomas.

After a while I was allowed to come down a bit. My head was all over the place: I was exhausted mentally but my body just kept on going no matter how wrung out it felt. There was something in my backside buzzing away, not so big it was uncomfortable and I have to admit that it was doing the business for me. Candace was watching me from a distance, sizing up my reaction to this new factor. I had to remember that having things poked up the bottom is bad for macho types, even though it wasn't exactly a new experience for me. I've carried messages up there before now, and rolls of film, and several years ago I had to infiltrate an outfit that had a homosexual experience as part of their initiation – that whole 'breaking down barriers' nonsense – so it wasn't really that big a deal. What I had to remember was that to the average hard man this was humiliating and the sort of thing used to destroy self-esteem, especially if the subject finds it pleasant. Candace had made sure that it would be pleasant, and I was grateful for the fact that she'd used plenty of lube.

Playing the part, I looked ashamed and she smiled indulgently at me.

'What's wrong? Does it feel nice?' I tried to nod. 'That's good. You're supposed to like it, because I want you to.' She stepped forward to stroke my face. Her touch was electric, a combination of my arousal and her perfume. Whoever was downstairs started work on me again, and my body jerked as they started playing with the appliance as well. It felt good, and the pressure was really building.

'It's going to be even better this time, because I say it will. You're going to be a good boy and come even harder for me. I want to hear you scream this time. Do you think you can scream for me?'

I didn't try to answer; everything else was too much again for me to concentrate. The assistant was really going for it and I couldn't have resisted if I'd tried. I was getting to a point where I didn't *want* to resist, just let the orgasm take me and clear my mind for a few minutes of clear thought. It felt like mere seconds before pleasure started to turn into pain again, that need for release knotting every muscle. Candace watched it all, smiling and nodding her approval.

'Are you ready?' I just about managed to nod, my teeth gritted and lips pulled back into a grimace. 'You know what to say,' she replied.

'Please . . . Mistress.'

'Good boy. Come . . . now.' As she finished the instruction I heard myself shout with the release of all that tension and I drifted into unconsciousness, my brain overloaded with the rush of sensation.

I don't know how long it took before Candace was

happy with me. The same procedure was repeated over and over again, with me blacking out at the end. For a while I was barely able to remember words, and only spoke when she prompted me. I stopped thinking about suicide, and went through a phase where I only wanted to hear her tell me I was a good boy.

After a while I discovered that Candace's assistant was female, because I was instructed to return the favours I'd been given. I was taught to perform every act imaginable, including some I'd never heard of. Then, finally, Candace kissed me. It was better than anything I'd ever known, a rush on an entirely different level. It was like a spiritual awakening that took me to places I'd only read about in books.

At last, I was removed from the restraints and allowed to kneel at my mistress's feet. She was pleased with me, and that made me happy. She said that she was going to put me to work soon. She would allow me to serve her properly. She lifted her skirt and told me to do as I'd been taught.

'What a good boy you are. A fine slave, even better than Annie was.'

Annie. I vaguely remembered the name. Something to do with my previous life. I put the thought aside and did as I had been told. My mistress grunted in approval of my service.

The name came back, though. Annie. It wasn't important, nothing could be as important as serving my mistress.

A memory surfaced, like something in the far distance: blood. Something to do with blood, and was there a knife in there somewhere?

Annie . . .

Annie was dead. Why did that matter? My job was to serve my mistress. My job was to protect my mistress from harm.

My job was to protect . . .

My job . . .

It hit me like a ton of bricks. Somehow I'd managed to hold on to myself, hiding my true identity deep inside even as Candace had worked her own particular brand of magic on me. Now I remembered. I pulled my tongue away from its place of work and bit. Hard.

Candace screamed in agony as I tasted blood. She grabbed my hair, trying to pull me loose, but I bit down a second time – harder than the first. Hands grabbed me from behind as the assistant came to her mistress's aid and I moved back with her, coming to my feet. The lack of resistance unbalanced her and I took the moment it gave me to grab her by the throat, spin her round and lock an arm around her shoulders. I repositioned the hand around her neck so she was in the crook of my elbow, then twist and pull, and there was a crunching sound as her spine snapped. I threw the body at Alder, giving me time to reposition myself.

'GET BACK ON YOUR KNEES!' Two minutes previously that would have been all it would have taken to stop me, but I was back in charge of myself and feeling particularly disobedient. A right hook met her jaw with a loud crack and I felt the bone give way.

'Shut the fuck up, Candace.' Blood was pouring from her mouth, a sight that made me very happy indeed. The pain from between her legs was making it difficult for her to stand up, so I caught her by the hair and launched her face first across the room. As she crumpled onto the floor I stamped down on the spot I'd bitten with my bare heel. That seemed to take her over the threshold, and her eyes rolled back into their sockets as the lids came down.

My impulse was to keep kicking, but there were more important things to worry about. I found the door out of the cell and investigated the house beyond. My car was in the garage, with keys in the ignition and a spare set of clothes in the back. It was the suit I'd got from Brutus, but it would have felt good to put on if it had been a sandpaper nappy.

I had an idea.

The kitchen yielded up a carving knife and a cook's blowtorch. Perfect for what I had in mind. I returned to the dungeon with my tools and got to work.

Half an hour later I was driving away from the house heading for London, leaving a blazing building in my wake.

I made two calls on the road: one to Brutus requesting an urgent meeting, and one to the Boss. It turned out that I'd been locked up for three weeks, and it took half an hour to convince him that it was still me. The news of Candace's death went a long way toward my rehabilitation, and I thanked whichever gods were listening that Candace's assistant was of an almost identical build. I'd made sure that the fire would make identification impossible, especially with all her teeth knocked out. I was to report to a safe house that evening for debrief, which gave me just enough time for my visit to Brutus.

'Hamlet, my man, you look like shit.' We were sitting

in his house taking afternoon tea. Birds were singing in the garden, and I suddenly felt very glad to be alive even if I wasn't looking my best.

'Thanks. It's been a rough couple of weeks.'

'I can buy that. Word was that you disappeared.'

'Call it an unexpected detour.'

'Right.'

'Tell me, Brutus, what would you say if I told you I'd brought you a present?'

'I'd ask what you wanted.'

'That you would.' I laughed. Laughing felt good. 'Seriously, this one's on me.'

'Now I'm curious.'

'Come take a look in the back of my car.' We walked out to where I'd parked on the drive, out of sight from the road and prying eyes. Brutus was wary, but humouring me right up until the point where I opened the boot.

'You have got to be kidding me. Is that what I think it is?'

'Yep. Think it's something that might interest you?'

'It might be, Hamlet. It might just be.' Candace was awake, and tried to say something, but nothing intelligible came out. 'There's a lot of people who'd like to talk to her.'

'I thought there might be. She's officially dead, and won't be capable of ordering people around, so with her protection gone she's an open target.'

Brutus was grinning his head off. 'Yeah, I heard about that. How did you manage . . . ?'

'Just think of it as the "Special Relationship" in action.'

The grin got even wider, and Brutus laughed out loud.

'And you're just giving her to me. No strings?'

'I figure being one up in your books might come in useful one day. Just make sure she has a really unpleasant time of it, will you?'

'Now that,' said Brutus, 'is something I can guarantee.'

By giving her to Brutus, I'd made sure that Candace would spend the rest of her life paying for what she'd done to me, and to Annie, and to everyone else whose lives she'd destroyed. She'd fucked with some powerful people over the years, and they'd be willing to pay Brutus large sums of money for the chance to entertain themselves at her expense. Since she wasn't able to talk, there was no chance that she'd be able to give orders or activate the triggers she'd left in their heads. It was fantasy payback, and something that would give me a little satisfaction every time I remembered her.

We chatted some more, and I caught up on what had been happening in my absence. It was the same old world in the same old state, so we swapped a few stories until it was time for Brutus to get ready for another night on the town and me to face the music for my absence.

Chapter Twenty-Three

I wasn't really expecting a warm reception after three weeks in the wilderness, and I wasn't disappointed. One minute I was standing by a bench between two lamp-posts and the next I was in the back of a van wearing handcuffs. At least they were smart enough to give recognition codes before I killed any of them, but not fast enough to prevent a broken arm and a dislocated shoulder for the snatch squad. It was their tough luck as far as I was concerned: I'd have gone quietly if they'd bothered to ask me nicely. Thanks to the unfriendly start it wasn't exactly a pleasant ride; even though I apologised immediately, and even offered to reset the shoulder, the other people in the van seemed to be hoping they'd have an excuse to subdue me before our journey was over. I had to disappoint them, though, and sat through the rest of the trip as quietly as a lamb.

After about an hour we pulled up outside a small country house and I was escorted into the drawing room, where the Boss was waiting for me. The contents of my pockets were presented to him in a plastic bag and I sat quietly in a chair while he sorted through them. It was bloody uncomfortable with my hands still cuffed behind my back, but I kept my mouth shut because I knew I was still getting the gentle treatment. If I gave them the excuse my condition would deteriorate very quickly indeed.

After my wallet, keys, penknife and weapons, the Boss finally came to the bloodstained white plastic bag. He held up the contents: a long strip of muscle, roughly cut at one end.

'And this is?' It was the first time he'd even acknowledged my presence.

'DNA sample, sir.'

'Whose?'

'Candace Alder's.'

'And what exactly is it?'

'Her tongue, sir. Figured that would be appropriate.'

'Indeed.' He passed it to Piers, who took it away – presumably for testing. 'So, where have you been?'

I told him the whole sorry story, edited to replace the corpse in the burned building as Alder's. There was no point hiding any of the details, even though they wouldn't do my career much good, since there were almost certainly psychics monitoring my thoughts as I spoke. There was no point hooking me up to a polygraph: I'd been taught how to beat them before I left basic training.

The trick to a convincing lie, and this applies to covers as well, is to believe it yourself. This is why deep-cover work is dangerous. Making yourself buy the bullshit is hard enough, but the really tricky part is knowing how to remember it's bullshit even though you believe it. I'd convinced myself of Candace's death on the way to the meeting, even to the point of feeling the satisfaction that came with her neck breaking in my arms. I felt that same rush when I told the Boss about it, and he seemed convinced.

'That's quite a tale,' he said once I'd finished. 'Why did you go to see Brutus?'

'To make sure you didn't have a contract out on me before I came in.' This was true, since Brutus would have mentioned it while I was there and it would have been rude to ask him straight out. The Boss nodded, accepting it as a reasonable enough precaution.

'What would you have done if we had?'

'Had this conversation from a distance, sir.'

That got an amused grunt. The phone rang and he answered it, presumably speaking to whoever was in charge of monitoring the debriefing.

'You seem to be telling the truth, no signs of hiding anything. Normally that would make me suspicious, but I think you're smart enough to know when not to shut up.' He walked across to my chair and unlocked the cuffs, then back behind the desk as I rubbed my wrists to get the circulation going again. 'You'll be wanting this.' He slid a folder across the desk towards me. 'Transcripts from the Sisters you captured. I don't want to know any more about what you did to Mooney, but she's going to be in hospital for a very long time.'

'She served her purpose, sir.'

'Yes, and not just for you either. Get some sleep, read that and I'll talk to you tomorrow.' He walked out, and a steward showed me to a bedroom. When I saw the bed I suddenly realised how tired I was, and only just managed to get my clothes off before sleep took me.

I woke up back on the rack in Candace's dungeon, with her smiling that evil smile of hers. The assistant was bobbing her head up and down between my legs again, each movement more excruciating than the last. Candace started whispering something in my ear that I couldn't hear, then reached up to open my mouth. She took a pair of pliers, pulled out my tongue and raised a large sharp knife . . .

And I was back in the house, sitting up in bed covered in cold sweat. I went through some breathing exercises to get my heart rate back under control, then tried to get some more sleep.

Candace brought the knife down across my tongue, slicing it cleanly away. I screamed incoherently as she pulled it free and put it into her own mouth, wiggling it a little to get it seated properly, then licked her lips with a smile. Her eyes flickered downwards to where the assistant continued her ministrations to my aching groin and she smiled again, wider this time. The mouth released me as Candace took a hold, raised the knife again . . .

And again I was sitting up in bed. This was not good. I summoned up the vision of me breaking her jaw, breaking her neck, then went on to smash her to tiny pieces in my mind. I took that image to sleep with me, and dreamed of inflicting violent revenge on Candace Alder with a smile on my sleeping face.

Breakfast consisted of coffee, bacon, eggs, toast and transcripts. It was all fairly standard cult stuff, and my guess was that they'd be in deprogramming for a while before they were allowed back in public. That was assuming they'd ever be released: they'd seen a little too much for civilians, and the shrinks would have to be sure there was no danger of them blabbing before it was signed off. Better to consider them dead, which was exactly what they'd be if they didn't make progress. We're blessed with some fairly impressive resources, but prison space isn't one of them.

What I wanted, of course, was to find Hamilton. She was now the only member of the Sisterhood remaining in the wild, and I wanted that particular species extinct. She'd been pretty firmly undercover since before Candace had taken me, but I assumed that they must have been in some kind of communication until her death. I swore quietly at myself for not making a decent search of the place before I torched it, since the phone records came up blank. If they'd been using unregistered cellphones I was out of luck, and would have to find some other means of tracking her down.

That evening I was allowed to leave the house, and made my way back to the old industrial unit to look at the records while I cleaned up and made it ready for the next occupant. I ran traffic analysis programs over all the communication records I could find, and every other kind of pattern hunting on the rest of it. Nothing useful came up.

My guess was she was hiding with her old red friends, but those that MI5 still had under surveillance showed no sign of having even spoken with her and those that had been considered unimportant were checked as well for good measure without success.

On the fourth day of fruitless searching I was startled by the telephone. The voice on the other end sounded uncertain, as though they had no idea who they were talking to.

'Hello? Um ... My name's Bert Wilson. I'm a security screener at Stansted Airport.'

'Yes, Bert, what can I do for you?'

'Well, I've just had this woman come through who looks like the woman on the poster I was given last month and it said I should call if I thought I'd seen her.'

'That's good, Bert.' I had no idea why the call had been put through to me, but decided to play along. I could always transfer him if it was useless, and it was a welcome break from racking my brains looking for data that I was becoming convinced wasn't there. I accessed the computer and found the option to tap into the airport's CCTV systems. 'Where was this, Bert?' He gave the location of the gate and it seemed to take hours to find the right image stream. I could see a nervous-looking man with hunched shoulders in one corner talking into a phone. 'All right, wave to the camera.' He did, and I could see it on the screen, confirming that I was in the correct place. 'Great stuff, I'm right with you now, Bert. How long ago was this?'

'About ten minutes. I've been on the phone since, explaining it to your colleagues.'

'That's the Civil Service for you, innit?' I was already rolling the footage back, looking at each face as they walked in front of the camera. 'Can you tell me what she was wearing?'

Bert rolled off the outfit like a professional, even down to the shoes and the bleached hair that really didn't work for her.

'It just looked wrong, like she'd spent so much effort on her appearance that she wouldn't have had hair that didn't fit, you know?'

'I know exactly what you mean, Bert.' Then suddenly I was looking at her. Bert was smack on the money: no self-respecting woman would have worn a suit that good and been seen in public without the hair just so. I took a good, long look, comparing it to the most recent photograph we had.

'Hello?'

'Sorry, Bert. I was looking at the image. Where is she now?'

'Her flight finished boarding just after she got on, but they're being held on the ground while I talk to you. We'll have to move them in a minute, though – I'm supposed to be pushing through a flight to Majorca now, and the queue's starting to get nasty.'

'All right, Bert, you hang tight and we'll take it from here. Good work, mate.'

I hit speed-dial and got the Boss.

'We've got Hamilton. She's just boarded a flight at Stansted.'

'Is that confirmed?'

'I'm looking at the camera footage now.'

'Then go get her.'

I reached Hereford in record time, and the helicopter took off while I was fastening my seatbelt.

London Stansted Airport was built at a time when the main threat to airline passengers came from hijacking and hostages rather than just blowing them up or flying them into things, and as such was designed with a holding area away from the main terminal for hijacked aeroplanes where they could be dealt with safely and not be in the way of normal airport operations. I could see a charter jet sitting on that spot as we made our approach, no doubt filled with unhappy holidaymakers wondering what was spoiling their fun.

Weapons were checked as we touched down, then the two helicopters pulled off again. We were in front of the cockpit, out of sight of the passengers, and the noise of our rotors and engines was masked by the aeroplane running its generators to keep power running inside. A perfect insertion to start, which made us all very happy. I gave a signal to the pilot and she switched from onboard to external power, closing down the engines so we could approach safely. A ladder unit moved into position with three buses behind it, ostensibly to transfer passengers to another aircraft since this one had a technical fault.

I made my way on board and played the part of a Nice Man in a Suit explaining what was going on and being ever so apologetic for the inconvenience. Nobody really pays attention to people like that anyway, and I shared a look with the flight attendant when the only question was about compensation. It was simple enough to split the passengers into four groups, and I'd made sure that Hamilton was in the last one so the wait for an extra bus would be a good excuse to filter her group out more slowly. One by one they came, until Hamilton brushed past me without recognition. We'd not met, so presumably my dark wig made me different enough from any pictures she might have seen. There were a few more passengers to get out, then I left the crew to wait until everyone was out of sight so they could move the aircraft into a position where it could pick all the passengers up again having been miraculously repaired.

At the bottom of the staircase, Hamilton seemed to be having trouble. Everyone else had their passports out ready for checking against the passenger manifest, but she couldn't find hers and it was causing a delay.

'Can I help?'

'My passport – I think it must have fallen out of my pocket.' Not quite, since it was currently sitting inside my jacket.

'That's OK, we'll go and look for it in a second.' I turned to the woman who was in charge of getting people onto the bus and sent her on her way. Soon it was just me, Hamilton and the strike team in overalls, the real technicians having been sent away quietly for a cup of tea.

'So, Miss . . . ?'

'Fraser. Will we be much longer?' She was looking nervous.

'Not at all, Miss Hamilton, I think we're pretty much done.' At the mention of her real name she went stiff and looked about for an escape route, but found that she'd been surrounded by armed men. 'Wouldn't you agree?' Her shoulders sagged and she bowed her head as one of the strike team stepped forwards with another set of handcuffs. As the first cuff went on, she kicked backwards and tried to step forwards to punch me. This would have worked beautifully if the man she'd kicked wasn't still holding on to the other end of the cuffs and her legs gave out as he pulled her backwards. Someone else stepped in to secure her, but I waved them back.

'Let's give the lady what she wants, shall we?' I grabbed Hamilton by the hair and punched her on the jaw. 'That's where I punched your girlfriend, you know. Broke her jaw so she couldn't try any of her mind-fuckery.' She was on all fours, climbing to her feet, so I kicked her in the stomach. 'You like that? You like being treated the way you treated your "Sisters"?' She was choking, the fight gone out of her, and I wasn't getting any satisfaction out of beating her anyway. I nodded to the team leader, and someone stepped in to roll her onto her back. She was secured at the wrists and ankles, then carried to the helicopter that had just landed about thirty feet away to begin a whole new life.

'So that's it.' The Boss was sitting behind another anonymous desk in another anonymous office, this time in a suburb just outside London.

'Yes, sir. Hamilton appeared to have lost her will to fight.'

'Eventually.'

'Yes, sir.' I shrugged.

'Good.' It was the closest I was likely to get to 'well done' or 'here, have a medal', but it would do.

'Take two weeks' leave, then come back in. I've got something else for you that should be a little more up your street.'

'Yes, sir. Thank you.' I left the office and stepped out into a clear morning, heading for a dingy little boozer where nobody asked questions. I needed to get drunk.

Coda

'You did *what?*'

'Sold her off through Brutus.' I was sitting in Kensal Green Cemetery again, catching up with Dead Geoff as I'd promised I would. Geoff laughed, a strange hissing sound that put my teeth on edge.

'Bloody hell, Jack, you know how to push your luck, don't you? What'll the Boss do if he finds out?'

'Kill me, most likely. You know how they feel about falsifying reports. Are you sure you've not got room for one more up here?'

'Not if it's you. You know there's another one of us up here now? They planted her yesterday. Nice service, very low key. I only twigged because the old man was there.'

'Yeah, that would have been Annie. Wish I could have been there myself.'

'Close, were you?'

'Not really, but you know what it's like. She went out on my watch.'

'Oh. Bugger. Well, she's over there somewhere.' Geoff waved towards the other side of the chapel. 'I said hello, but I think she's still adjusting.'

'I hear it's a lot to take in.'

'Yeah.'

We talked about old times, and the Sisterhood. My

nightmares came up, but they were already getting better after a week and I was reasonably confident that I'd be able to deal with them myself rather than face the shrinks. I don't like shrinks: they ask too many questions. Judging from Alder's established behavioural patterns she wouldn't have shared any trigger words that might have been implanted, which meant I was probably safe. The only person she was likely to have told was Hamilton, and poor Sadie wouldn't be talking to anyone for a very long time.

I poured myself another Scotch and topped up Geoff's glass. While he wasn't exactly drinking it, he was wafting his nose over it occasionally and the drink seemed to evaporate in his general direction. I wasn't that worried about the details, since he looked happy enough. Perhaps it was the company. He'd said he wasn't exactly snowed under with visitors. It didn't really say much for me, come to think of it; if the best company you can muster on a Saturday night is a dead guy, there's probably something wrong with your social life. Strangely enough, I see more of Geoff since he's pegged it than I did when he was alive; now it's just my schedule we have to contend with instead of wrestling with his as well. So my best mate's dead, but at least I've still got someone to talk to.

'Hello,' said Geoff, 'we've got company.'

I looked up and saw Annie crossing the graveyard towards us. She was looking good: hair in place and nicely dressed, moving with an increasing confidence. She certainly looked a lot better than the last time I'd seen her.

I smiled at her and raised a hand. 'Hey there.'

'Hello, Bill.'

'Bill's as dead as you are. Deader, in fact.'

'Then what shall I call you?'

'At this point you can call me Jack. Fancy a drink?' I smiled and waved the bottle at her. She looked confused, and Geoff explained the whole wafting/inhaling thing to her. It still didn't make any sense to me, but I wasn't dead. Not yet, anyway.

'Yes,' said Annie, 'I think I fancy a drink.' I topped up my glass and put it where she'd have easy access. She wrinkled her nose a little when I took a swig from the bottle.

'Don't tell me you're afraid of catching something.'

'Sorry, force of habit.'

'It's fine. One thing's still puzzling me, though, and I was hoping you'd have an answer. Just what the hell were the Sisterhood trying to accomplish? It's not as if they were going to overthrow the government just by whacking one person, even if it was the Prime Minister. Governments go on, you know? It's what they do.'

'They told me it was about stopping us from being involved in all the stupid little bush wars we get caught up in. Well, they said "responsible for" and "started", but you know what I mean: all that crap the Americans seem so keen on getting us to help with.'

I laughed my head off as things clicked into place. 'That explains the other group. They were a mix from all over Europe: different outfits, different ideologies. The only thing they had in common was a connection to leftist politics. Killing for peace and all that.'

Two confused expressions were pointing at me.

'The name of the trigger group: Eleven-Eleven?' I shook my head sadly and despaired of the education system. 'The eleventh of November nineteen eighteen. An anniversary celebrated all over the world.'

'Armistice day,' said Geoff.

'The end of the First World War.' Annie's eyes were wide, probably kicking herself for not spotting it before.

'Precisely.' Now that I'd said it, the faint echoes of Vaclav and Alexei's memories confirmed my conclusion. I hadn't mentioned that part to Geoff, since the spike had given him the willies when he was alive. I imagine he'd be even less keen on a thing that eats souls now, although part of me wonders from time to time what would happen if I used it on a ghost. Time to change the subject.

'Good funeral, was it?'

'Yeah, I suppose,' replied Annie. 'Had a pretty good turn-out, given it took a while to release my body and get the thing organised. Whole piles of relatives I haven't seen in years, of course. I always got dragged to see obscure relatives off so it's nice to know the rest of them turned out for me. Shame you weren't there, though.'

'I was busy.' In fact I'd spent the previous two days with a couple of professional ladies and a crate of booze, making sure that Candace hadn't done any permanent physical damage. To me it was an essential check on working equipment, and I've always said check and check again. Annie was still talking.

'The Boss showed up, though, and that greasy little monkey of his.'

'Piers,' said Geoff and I together, and all three of us laughed.

'The Boss was really nice, spoke to my mother and said how horrible it was about the accident. He even bothered to tell her that I was popular in the office, that I shouldn't have worked so hard and how guilty he felt about my falling asleep at the wheel on my way home after another late night at work. He was convincing, too. I almost fell for it and I was there when it happened!'

'Yeah. Sorry about that.' I was.

'Not much you could have done. My real personality was trying to assert itself but Caroline's – Candace's – programming was laid in too strongly. It's just a pity Sharon was there as well.'

'I should have shot her first.'

'That would have just closed me down completely. I'd have probably killed myself then, to stop you taking me. At least this way I left all of that nonsense behind.'

'I suppose so. Doesn't mean I have to like it, though.'

'Can't say I was planning on dying young myself.'

'Me neither,' said Geoff. 'Not our bloody choice though, is it?'

That led to an uncomfortable silence for a bit, so I picked up my guitar and played the blues for a while.

'That's nice,' Annie said quietly. 'You should be a musician. I really liked it when you were playing at that pub.'

'Sometimes I am.' I rattled off the names of a couple of people I'd played for that would have made the Bristol mob go nuts. Annie had even heard of one of them. Oh, sweet youth. We sat there in silence as I ran through a couple more numbers, then I refilled the glasses and took stock of what remained in the bottle. Not much, since we'd been sitting there for a while.

'You know,' I said, looking at Annie, 'I can't exactly call you "Annie" any more, can I?'

'I suppose not.'

'So what should I—'

'My name is – was – is? Anyway, it's Sophie. Sophie Henderson.'

'Well, here's to you, Sophie.' I drained the last of the bottle and resisted the urge to throw it at a gravestone. The last time I did that I got six months of nagging from the owner.

'All right, you two, enough of the warm and fuzzy shit.' Geoff grinned. 'Let's go and watch some Goths shagging.'

So that's exactly what we did. I even managed to nick their booze while they were busy.

Another day, another anonymous building. Some of the great landmarks of the City of London rose around me as I walked towards my meeting with the Boss. Up another flight of stairs, down another corridor, into another broom cupboard. He was there, same as always, waiting behind his desk with a cup of tea and a plain brown envelope between us.

'Enjoy your leave, did you?'

'Yes, sir, thank you.'

'Feeling refreshed? Ready for the next one?' A pointless question, since he had the final say about whether I was ready or not and my input on the matter was invited as a pointless attempt to make me feel better about it. I could have been sitting there with one lung and no limbs, but if he said I was off, then off I would go.

'Absolutely, sir.' That got the formal bullshit out of the way, at least. Now we could get on with the business part.

'Good. Got a group of druids down in Somerset who've

been getting a bit frisky. Looks like they might be trying to wake Arthur up to save us from our corrupt leaders.'

'I imagine Her Majesty would prefer not to share the throne, sir, even with him.'

'Well, I can't speak for her, but I know I'd rather it didn't happen. Make sure it doesn't.'

'Sir.'

'Background.' He pulled the folder out of its envelope and threw it across to me. It was yet another red one.

What a surprise.